DECEITFUL WOLF

FATED OBSESSION
BOOK 1

ALLIE SANTOS

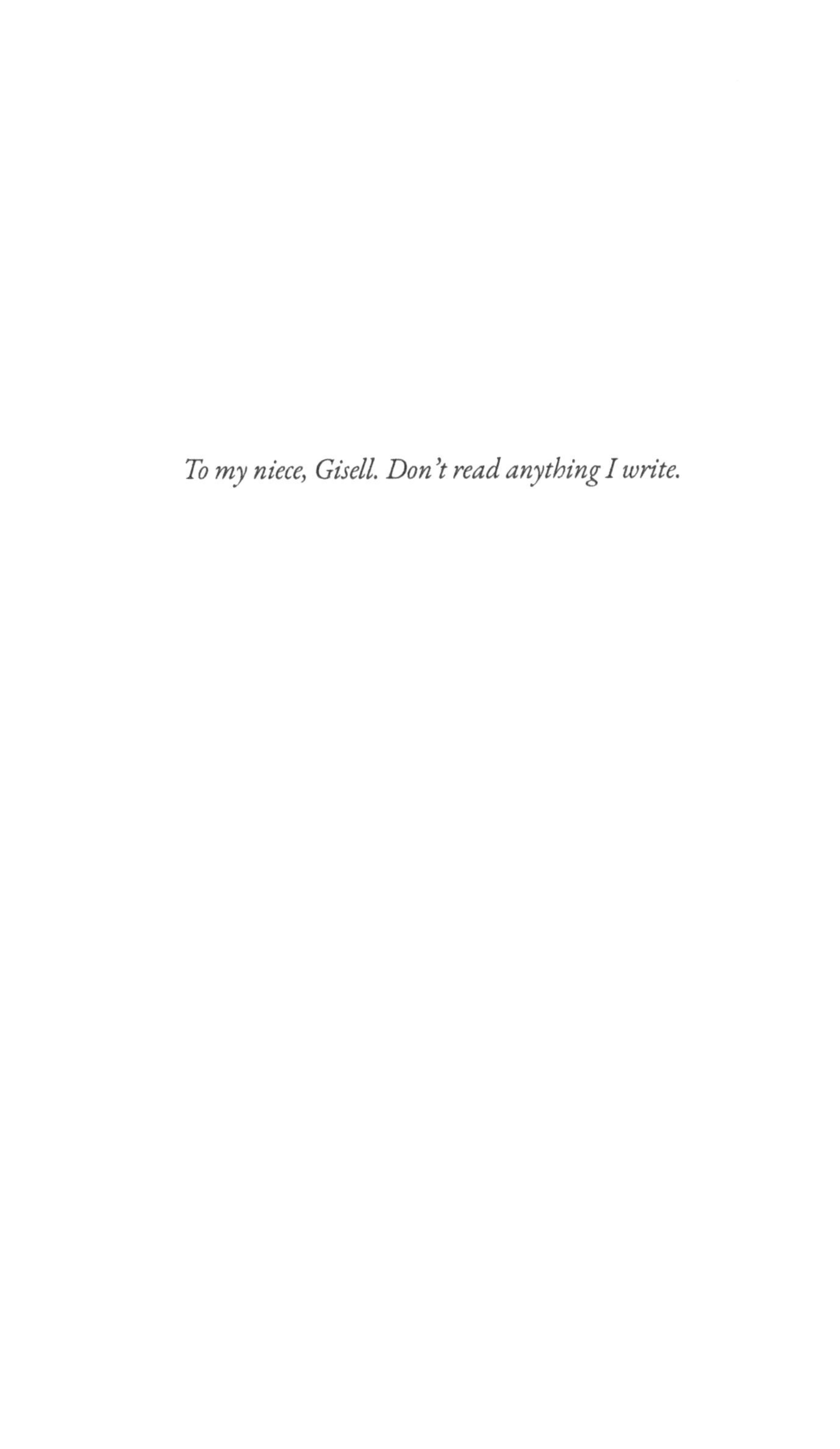

To my niece, Gisell. Don't read anything I write.

A NOTE FROM ALLIE

This series will follow the girls from the Fae Queen series finding their fated mates. If you have no idea what that means, you can start the trilogy with Kiss of Fate. You don't have to, but it will give you an insight on what they lived through before the start of this book.

There will be references to characters that have their own books, so for maximum enjoyment, I recommend that the *Fated Obsession* series be read in order.

Love,
Allie 🤍

CONTENT WARNINGS

Violence, Captivity, Murder on Page, Enemies-to-Lovers, Angst, Other Woman Drama

Please be advised that the following trigger and content warnings contain spoilers for the story and plot of the novel.

Deceitful Wolf is an M/F Paranormal Romance. The MMC is cruel to his fated mate at the beginning of the story because of his trauma. There is no cheating.

Deceitful Wolf is set in a mythical world and all contents are purely fiction.

CHAPTER 1
CAMILLA

"No, my dear country bumpkin, I'm going to dare you to . . ." Eliza paused for dramatic effect.

Oh, no, what was she going to have me do now? I seriously needed to stop betting her on things. This one was all on me, too. But I was so sure the bet we'd made on our mutual friend's relationship was going to last longer than two months, but their sexual chemistry had sizzled.

Eliza *had* to be getting insider information.

My attention was drawn back to Eliza when she hummed. "Ask a man out."

My shoulders dropped with relief. It could have been worse, but still, that first time was embarrassing as all heck.

"You already did that to me." I drew out my words, hoping she'd pity me, but I knew my bestie. She wasn't about to relent. When she got stuck on a dare, she was a bull.

Rae laughed from her spot and as she lifted her drink. I shot her a dirty look, but she was too busy chugging alcohol to catch it.

"I did, but it was my mistake letting you choose whom to

ask," Eliza said, giving me a look. "This time, it's going to be a red-blooded, alpha man. Not that shy bird you chose. He could hardly speak in the presence of your gorgeousness."

My head dropped onto the rim of my glass. I'd rather help a cow give birth than deal with a man who thought his way was God's truth. Yet, that had been my experience with the alpha types, which was why I stayed far, far away.

"That one." She'd already picked him out!?

I kept my head down, hoping everything would disappear. That this was all a figment of drunken scenarios my mind had conjured. What had probably happened was I got absolutely obliterated so Rae had to carry me home and this was some weird manifestation. Plus, it would be an easy thing for Rae to tote us around now that she had super strength and a slew of other nifty abilities.

"Wow, their eyes are super cool," Rae muttered.

"You can see their eyes?" Eliza exclaimed.

Rae shushed her. Jennie was here. We couldn't have her knowing Rae was far from human. Or that anything remotely Unnatural existed. It was still crazy to me that the supernatural world was real, and on top of that, they were actually called Unnaturals.

Fae, vampires, and werewolves weren't supposed to exist, but that was far from the truth. According to Rae, every creature we'd ever heard about in myths or legends actually existed in some way or another. I shivered, and the rim of my drink dug deeper into my forehead.

"Details, please," Eliza said in a significantly lower tone.

"The scowling one has green eyes and the other one has hazel," Rae murmured.

My lady bits perked up and peeked over the fence I'd

corralled them behind in the last months. I stamped the hoe hormones down. Alpha-looking *and* colored eyes? I was screwed, and I hadn't even turned around.

"Ooo, that sounds interesting," Eliza breathed. "I want you to ask for the scowling guy's number."

Her words registered as I chastised my hormones.

I shot up and slammed my hand on the table, heart thudding.

"What?" I refused to think it was from excitement. Rae laughed at me, and Eliza snorted. Eliza was trying to get me out of the funk I'd been in since graduation closed in on me. Now that frantically studying for finals was over, I should have been relieved, yet it was the opposite. I'd graduated with an accounting degree I loathed, and I had no idea where to go from here.

I scowled at my glass before eyeing their drinks. They were off their rockers. Maybe they needed to be cut off.

"You heard me, the one with green eyes. He seems like what your type should be. All burly and muscly and a bit scary-looking. You need a good tossing about by the caveman type. Loosen you up from all that studying you did." Called it. She was always looking out for me, and right now, she wanted me to loosen up in a way I hadn't in a minute.

"You sound intrigued, *you* go ask him," I grumbled.

"Nope. That's the bet. Plus, I don't mesh with the whole caveman bit. I need a bit more control. Don't think you're distracting me. You have two minutes to get your butt over there to ask."

I glared at her. "You are evil."

"Hi, these drinks were sent over by the two gentlemen over

there." A tray clapped on the table, and the waitress strutted off in a hurry.

My eyebrow arched as I surveyed the five drinks identical to the ones I purchased. I itched to turn and look at the table, but I forced myself to stay still. I couldn't give Eliza more ammunition.

"There you go, Camilla. They see something they like over here. I think you'll be okay," Rae said as she sipped one. It could have been ambrosia for all I knew because a heartbeat later, she was chugging it.

"That good?" Jennie said, eyeing Rae. After taking a swig, she grimaced. "Uh, no, they taste horrid."

They debated as I eyed one of the frothy cups in front of me. Curious, I gripped one and tilted it into my mouth for a sip. The explosion of fruits hit my tongue. It was delicious. The ones I'd ordered had nothing on these. But as good as they were, Rae's reaction was startling. My slightly tipsy mind noticed she was acting like she'd just gotten her hands on the Holy Grail and was drinking the liquid of immortality. I chuckled under my breath as I thought about the stories my brother obsessed over.

I studied my drink and was about to push it away until I recalled the dare. I stretched my neck from side to side. Liquid courage, coming up. I hadn't even seen what he looked like. After all, they could be messing with me, and he was uglier than my Uncle Earl.

Either way, alcohol would do me a solid. Eliza slid a second glass to me as I finished and thumped the empty cup on the table.

"You got this." Eliza slapped me on the back, and I side-eyed her as I contemplated pulling her luscious red hair.

"Go, go, go," Rae chanted, slightly slurred, her lips spread in a grin. Ouch, Rae, not making it any better for me. I'd expected her to be on my side, but she was headlong intoxicated. The only perk from watching Rae act like a total lush? Knowing fae still got drunk.

I ran my hands down my clothes, trying to dry the sweat. No more stalling. Time to get a phone number. I twisted on the heels of my cowgirl boots. My gaze bounced over the multitude of people and settled toward the back corner of the bar. *My goodness*, he was hot. No, not simply hot. Mouthwatering. My body perked up, and I swallowed hard.

Get a hold of yourself. I squeezed my fluttering hands to my sides and tilted up my chin. He was all-around bad news. I could see it from here. I roved my eyes over him as I neared. He was *huge*. Alarmingly so, but at the same time, in the best ways. In an 'I want to climb all over him and have him toss me around' type of way.

I stopped my hand from fluttering to my wavy hair as his shadowed eyes settled on me. The arms he had crossed on his chest were so huge, I was positive I wouldn't be able to wrap my hand around the bicep. From the excited dip in my stomach, my body begged for his touch.

I'd been in a drought, and all those emotions and sensations pulsed to the surface. I liked sex—a lot, and I'd been without it for a couple of months after breaking up with Jaden.

Life after being kidnapped and taken to Faerie had leased a new perspective, so I'd chosen to give an actual relationship a try. I should have just stuck to meaningless week-long affairs instead of wasting my time. The relationship had lasted a few months, but little had I known it had been based on lies. I chalked up my stupidity to the fact that I'd been held captive for weeks on end. Like a glutton for punishment, my memory called on that particular pile of dung.

One second, I'd been happily striding down the street, minding my own business, and the next, some psychotic man had kidnapped me. The only thing was, he didn't turn out to be a man, but instead a fae. I was held captive in Faerie for months, which was even longer in the human world. It had been a crazy, scary, and stressful experience, but at least I'd survived it, which couldn't be said for everyone who had been captured. As if it wasn't enough, I found out that I carried the dormant fae gene, and if magic was around, I would have immediately become fae when I turned twenty-two, which was only weeks away.

There was still a chance of that happening if Rae ever managed to figure out a way to free bound magic. It was her one goal as the newly minted fae Queen. It all sounded like a bunch of drama. Either way, I was taking life by the horns as a fae or a human. Rae being fae tremendously dulled the fear of turning.

As fear riddled as my experience in Faerie had been, I didn't regret it. I met my-ride-or-die Eliza, as well as the rest of the girls. It was like I gained a slew of sisters.

I weaved around some rowdy groups and stepped up the ramp, my cowboy boots clicking with every step, amplifying my anxiety at asking a stranger for his number. Sure, I'd done it before. But never someone like *him*.

I should have taken up Jeremy's offer when he reached out a week ago. Jeremy, my classmate, had been my tame rebound after I found out how much of a fool I'd been with Jaden. How blind I'd been, quick to believe lies. Or maybe, like Eliza joked, I just had a thing for guys that names started with the letter J. The thing was, Jeremy didn't get the job done. I mean, he was nice and sweet, but there was this edge of dissatisfaction. I wished the softer ones did it for me… but it was just blah.

The big guy's friend leaned back, making my eyes fall on him. He seemed much more laid-back if the half-smile on his face was any indication, and he was by no means small. Goddammit! Why couldn't he have been the target? He seemed more relaxed than the other.

"Howdy, y'all," I chirped, sauntering up to the round table. When the heavy eyes settled on me, I had to bite my tongue so it didn't roll out. Up close, they were piercing and a deep mossy green.

Green eyed man grunted.

"Daniel Lyons." His friend tipped his head in hello. "Did y'all like the drinks Greyson and I sent over?" Daniel's drawl was syrupy and, in its own right, damn enticing, but why couldn't I take my gaze off the guy with green eyes?

"They were delicious, I've never had anything like it." I crossed my arms and jutted my hip to the side, trying to get green eyes to look at me, but he remained impassive.

"We had something extra put in them," Greyson finally said without the southern accent his friend had. The deep rumbling voice was shiver-inducing.

"Were y'all trying to drug a whole group of girls?" I teased.

Greyson tensed, suddenly alert. The pissed look on his face morphed to suspicion, and he opened his mouth, but his friend beat him to it.

"We asked them to infuse it with strawberry mango syrup. My sister swears by it."

As if out of a trance, I settled my eyes back on Daniel. Greyson grunted and straightened with a scowl that smoothed out just as quick as it appeared. The mention of a sister made me relax, and I grinned. I never thought to mix it into drinks. That was going to be my new go-to.

"So, you liked it?" Greyson eyed me critically, a stilted smile spreading his mouth.

"It was divine," I said. It was obvious he was forcing himself to be cordial. Maybe he liked what he saw when he looked at me, but wasn't much of a seducer? Another possibility was that he didn't want me, and I was too cocky for my own good.

I prepared to ask him for his number and skedaddle back to my group, but then his gaze slanted down to my breasts. His gaze was like a physical touch, and my nipples hardened. I pressed my lips together so I didn't grin.

"Sit," he demanded and nodded to the empty seat next to him.

My shoulders tensed in irritation, and my teeth clicked together. The tone was *not* working for me. The order was equal parts irritating and arousing. I wasn't about to give up, though. I'd lost the bet and damned if I didn't fulfill my payment. Daniel sighed, and the chair screeched on the ground as he got to his feet and brought my eyes to him. I'd been staring at Greyson as I'd processed the rioting contradictions swirling in my gut.

"I'll be going," Daniel said with a smirk, squeezing Greyson's shoulder as if warningly. My eyebrows furrowed, but I shrugged off the bro vibe they had.

As soon as his friend made his escape, I shot a look at the table where my group sat in time to see Rae leaving with a cute All-American type. I should get back to see who that snack was and why he was dragging Rae with him. Turning back to green eyes, I opened my mouth to ask for his number, but he gripped my wrist in a smooth motion and pulled me down to the chair.

Fortunately, my butt was properly padded, so it didn't hurt when I thumped down. The strange dichotomy of emotions made a showing. Anger and lust swirled and whatever I was going to snap became stuck in my throat.

As a lock of my hair swung to the front of my face, Greyson angled forward and brushed it behind my ear. "What's your name?"

"Camilla Richardson." My breath caught as he got in my bubble. I wanted him. Bad. The raw maleness he exuded called to every fantasy I'd had. A shuddered breath left me, and his eyes lit up with smugness. I pressed my thighs together.

"Camilla." Greyson's eyes flashed to mine, and my stomach erupted into flutters. Shit, he was bad news. My lady parts' reaction told me I was in deep cow shit. His large hand slid to the back of my neck and clasped it. It made my hackles rise, but at the same time, it made me want to climb into his lap and rub myself all over him.

I'd never reacted so viscerally. It was startling and yet thrilling. This was the sexual connection I'd been searching for —one I had never fully grasped.

"You're very touchy for someone I just met." My eyebrow winged up as anger and desire nipped at my heels. Angry sex didn't sound too bad right about now.

Setting my hands on his leg, I leaned closer. Every muscle in Greyson's neck tensed. He liked what he saw. The plan had been to simply get his number, but...

Something quick couldn't hurt, right? A little relapse for the bad boy—just for one night.

CHAPTER 2
GREYSON

EARLIER

THIS WAS FUCKING RIDICULOUS. I HAD BETTER things to do than to wait around in a bar because of fucking fae.

"Is Tristin positive that the scent was the new Fae Queen's?" I asked.

Daniel patted his pocket where he held the scrap of clothing infused with the smell we tracked to this very bar.

"Yes," Daniel huffed, exasperated. I eyed the group of girls striding toward the table in the middle of the bar. "You smell it from that group, too?"

Ever since magic was bound decades ago, my werewolf senses had been restricted, but I was still able to track. It was nothing like I would be capable once magic was back and I had my heightened senses, but at least I wasn't useless.

"Yes," I said gutturally, studying the five girls. My eyes switched to each, but I couldn't pinpoint which one it was. All Unnaturals were known for their beauty. Other than that, there was nothing distinct that indicated fae other than their ears and all of these girls had their ears covered by masses of hair.

I sneered. I would need to get closer so I could scent the fae.

One girl with dark cowgirl boots and a curvy waist separated from the group, and my eyes narrowed on her. The curve of her ass begged for my hand while I gripped the dark hair falling down her back.

Disgust filled me. She could be the fae and I lusted after her?

"Which one is it?"

"I don't know." Daniel brushed his brown hair back, eyeing the group diligently.

"Here," I said, sliding a flask of wolfsbane toward Daniel. His eyebrows flicked up, and he whistled low. "It'll be abhorrent to humans. We can single *it* out that way."

"Have I told you you're my hero, Alpha?"

I growled in answer at the title because that's all it was, an archaic title that had no meaning since magic was gone.

"I'll be back," Daniel drawled.

The cool beer on the table sweated and gathered a ring of water beneath it. Unable to help myself, I admired the girl with the boots as she moved away from the bar, drinks balanced in her hands, smiling at a male flirtatiously as she left. My hands fisted, and I sneered down at them. Fucking fae ruined everything. I could be at home, not here, watching some girls.

If I weren't desperate to get magic back, I would have told Daniel to chase his nonsensical leads himself. But I *was* desperate, and if there was some truth to the scrap of clothing that allegedly held the scent of the Queen whose death would bring magic back, then I had no choice but to try for my pack— no, my species.

Tristin had reached out to Daniel with the tip.

Alphas from other regions never communicated with one another, especially since magic was bound and our wolves were trapped within our human bodies. We kept to our designated areas, holding onto the traditions of the old ways that had become lost.

"Done, I ordered some of the same drinks they had and slipped the wolfsbane in," Daniel said, sliding into his chair.

"We need to get on with this," I snapped, itching to get out of here. Being around so many humans unsettled me. I preferred the quiet of my lands.

"You're such a grumpy old fucker."

A growl rumbled in my chest. "You're the same age as me, mutt."

We met as pups three hundred and sixteen years ago and since his father had been my father's beta, we'd grown up together. Daniel was the one person I trusted. He'd seen me at my worst and best and remained beside me.

"Yet, I wear my age with grace and wisdom." Daniel went quiet, and his next words made me stiffen. "Do you think the old ways will come back if we free magic?"

"I don't know." There was too much unknown. Without our wolves' instincts, we'd fallen out of the pack hierarchy werewolves used to have. Slowly but surely, wolves had dispersed.

There were few full werewolves and another few descendants of werewolves that had never matured and lived out their human lives on my land. Each Alpha from varying locations handled the disappearance of magic differently, but I refused to force anyone to stay. Especially after failing to protect them a long time ago. For those that wanted to remain, I offered them a safe place to live, as well as protection for as long as they were loyal to me.

I was lucky to have reached twenty-two and cemented into

immortality years before magic was bound. Else, I would have lived out my life as a human as I'd witnessed others experience too many times to count.

"They received the drinks." At Daniel's words, I turned back to the group of girls and watched one take a sip and then begin chugging it down. "That one."

Satisfaction filled me as I eyed the dark-haired girl in a leather jacket. Her hair was over her ears, but the way she drank the concoction told me everything I needed to know. Confusion furrowed my eyebrow as a blonde pushed the drink toward Boots with disgust. Boots tipped the drink and chugged it.

"Fuck, two of them," Daniel muttered.

"At least we get to get rid of more fae," I said, shrugging. Boots finished chugging the drink down like it was some type of drug, which technically it was.

"What if one is matured?" The shock in Daniel's voice made me tense. Tristin had also passed on that little tidbit about the humans who would turn fae once magic was free. Waiting in the sideline to fill the world with more disgusting, traitorous fae. The not matured one would be easier to take down since she would currently be human.

"Parasites," I sneered. "Fae disguised as human." If I had access to my wolf form, I'd be able to track every fucking fae and tear them to pieces.

"One is coming this way." The excitement in Daniel's voice jarred me from my bitter thoughts. "I can get her to come home with us."

I stifled the growl in my chest at the cocky words.

That plan was shot to shit when she settled her pretty browns on me. They were framed with sooty lashes that made the pupils pop. I shifted uncomfortably as she raked her eyes over me. Desire flicked in the depths. As she neared, she smelled and seemed human. This must be the one with the dormant gene then.

"Shit, she's going for you. Grey, I know you have a thing for being a dick, but we need her. If she's not the Queen, then she's eventually going to turn. Fifty-fifty chance. She had to know something. That group seems close."

I agreed. Either way, one of these dirty fae was leaving with me tonight.

"Hi, y'all," Boots chirped with a slight twang as she strutted up confidently. A soft smile spread across her face, and her eyes met mine. I grunted, pissed that my dick took notice of her curves.

"Daniel Lyons," Daniel said, introducing himself. "Did y'all like the drinks Greyson and I sent over?"

I barely held back my growl because he offered our real names. Idiot.

"They were delicious. They didn't taste like the ones I bought," she said, fiddling with the bangle on her wrist. Her skin was a golden brown, and her features were unmistakably hispanic. I took in tight jeans that hugged her rounded hips. The shirt she wore was frilled at the bottom and hugged her. I fisted my hands so I didn't reach out and place them on the indent of her waist.

"We had something extra put in them," I said without thinking.

"Were y'all trying to drug a whole group of girls?" she teased. *Shit.*

"We asked them to infuse it with strawberry mango syrup.

My sister swears by it," Daniel said quickly and nudged me under the table. I grimaced.

She relaxed when Daniel mentioned a nonexistent sister. Shit, why couldn't she show interest in him? He was smooth with women. They loved him and that southern charm he had going on. I was always too blunt and demanding. Women didn't mind it when I had them in bed, but this one needed finessing.

I tried to relax my shoulders and forced myself to smile. "So, you liked it?"

"It was divine," she said, and the way she watched me made me want to take her then and there. She wanted me to do it if the way she eyed me and licked her lips was any indication. I noted her thighs squeezing together.

Fuck . . . I forcibly ignored my hardening cock.

"Sit," I said roughly, nodding my head to the empty seat next to me. I watched her shoulders draw up, and fire sparked in her eyes. She didn't like being ordered around, but still, raw desire flushed her face. I could use that anger to my advantage.

Daniel sighed, and the chair screeched on the ground as he got to his feet. "I'll be going."

His hand settled on my shoulder with a squeeze. We'd been together long enough to know each other's moves. I'd noted the other girl at their table who'd drunk the wolfsbane being led out. He was telling me he was going to follow.

I watched Boots as she glanced behind her, and I braced myself before I gripped her wrist and pulled her to sit. Her hair swung forward, and I gave into my desire to brush it back. It was in the name of seducing her.

If I kept thinking that, maybe it would be true.

"What's your name?"

Her breath caught. "Camilla Richardson."

Her throat worked as she swallowed and a flush stained her neck. If I reached to touch her pussy, she'd be ready for me. I leaned close. She shuddered, and I couldn't help the smug satisfaction. My dick swelled, thick and needy. Fuck, it'd been a while. After this, I was going to have to visit Tara.

"Camilla," I rasped as my hand slid to her neck and squeezed. I'd never felt a need this potent. That fire flashed in her eyes again, urging on my hard-on. Her little tongue flicked out and wet her lower lip.

I fucking wanted her. *No*, I wanted a woman. Any would do. She was just here.

"You're very touchy for someone I just met." Camilla pressed her hand on my thigh, near my cock, making it twitch toward her. I stifled a groan.

"I want to touch you," I rasped, wishing I didn't mean it, but fuck, I did.

My cell vibrated in my pocket, and I pulled it out in a swift motion, angling it away from Camilla. I glowered down at the text message. *The girl left with a fae. It was her.*

It was a slap in the face. Fuck, we missed out on the Queen.

Camilla stretched, brushing her hand through her hair next to me. She had to know something about all of this. She was obviously not human.

I'll take the other one to the house. I texted Daniel back and prepared myself for kidnapping the woman in front of me.

"Come home with me." I tipped her chin up, and the desire in her eyes flared. I had her, but what worried me was that she had me, too.

CHAPTER 3
CAMILLA

I BIT MY TONGUE TO HOLD IN MY WHIMPER. GREYSON was desire incarnate. His thumb pressed into my chin, and he leaned in to take my mouth. And just like that, I was a goner. His lips were demanding, and when he nipped my lower lip, I almost came from that alone. All my pent-up desire burned beneath my skin.

Pulling back slightly, I met his mossy eyes, half-lidded with desire. Doubt flittered through me for a split second. The very idea of going home with him made me tense.

My experience of being kidnapped had left its scars. The fear wasn't foreign, but I'd worked hard at dispelling it. That's why the girls and I had a code if we were in danger. Exhaling sharply, I pushed my reservations to the side.

"Okay," I breathed, licking my lips and pressing close. As I flicked my tongue into his mouth, a stampeding herd erupted in my stomach.

My goodness, he was a wonderful kisser.

Greyson's hand gripped my waist and pulled me to stand in

an easy motion. My heart stuttered in my chest at the ease he handled me.

My wide eyes fell on the table where I could see the girls gaping at me sans Rae. Eliza's red hair bounced as she waved her hands in the air. She was probably satisfied by the turn of events.

I pulled my cell out from my back pocket. *I'm going home with him.*

Eliza got back to me in seconds. *Ride him like a bull, cowgirl.*

I bit my lip, so I didn't grin.

Oh, I intended to.

"Ready?" I chirped, looking up at him.

Greyson's hand went to my hair again, and he brushed it behind my ear. He fiddled with the shell, which sent shudders down my back.

"Let's go to my place."

I followed after him, floating on pure lust. I hoped we made it to his place before I gave into him. Once outside, fresh air brushed my cheek, and the gravel crunched under my boots as he led me to a huge black truck. I eyed it, intrigued. There was a good amount of room to get round one done in there.

He helped me into the seat and, be still my heart, buckled me in before he slammed the door and moved to the driver's side. "I live a bit out of the way, so it's going to be a drive."

"As long as you don't try to murder me," I joked. That kind of worry was serious, but I had a pretty good bad-dude meter, and he wasn't throwing off any signals. Anyway, our code word along with the tracking devices on our phones, added another layer of safety. I was sure Eliza would be signing into the app to see where I was and take a screenshot of the location as we'd planned.

"Not yet," he said with a smirk. Oh, he had a sense of humor under all that moodiness.

We were on the road in moments. I reached for the stereo as he turned onto the freeway, and I flipped through the stations until I reached a familiar song. I moved to the upbeat melody, humming.

He eyed me from the corner of his eyes and a smile twitched up the corner of his lips. When the truck turned onto a private road, I unbuckled my seatbelt and gave into the need to press the side of my body next to his. One of the various perks for three-seater trucks.

Greyson tensed for a second before relaxing and swinging his arm over my shoulders to tuck me closer to him. A shiver coasted down my spine. He made me feel so tiny when I was near him. My sensitive breast pressed against his side, and I ached to get even closer.

The alcohol was now fully out of my system, making my earlier confidence simmer, but fuck it, I was here now, and I wanted to have fun. More specifically, I wanted him. I trailed my finger over his arm and down his chest. In the dim light of the car, I couldn't make out how my touch affected him until I grazed my fingertips over his zipper.

A harsh shudder passed over him, and my desire took the reins. This was the craziest thing I'd ever done, but I couldn't help myself in his presence.

I'd always been impulsive. I palmed his hard cock and deftly unbuttoned his pants.

"What are you doing?" he said with a growl.

Time to discover if he was a boxers or briefs type of guy.

I slipped the zipper down, and he sprung out, huge and hard. The tip engorged and rosy. My mouth watered.

Well . . . he was neither. The discovery made me wiggle uncomfortably into the seat as I adjusted to lean down. Jeez, he had the prettiest cock I'd ever seen.

"W—" Whatever he was going to say cut off on a hiss when I slid my lips over the head. A guttural groan rumbled in his chest, and I flicked my tongue over the tip, swirling it.

The truck rumbled as he pressed on the gas. With a smooth dip of my neck, I slipped my lips around him until I couldn't fit him anymore at this angle. I moaned, enjoying the feel of him jerking in my mouth.

"What the fuck?" he rasped.

I heard a creak, and I could have sworn the steering wheel cracked.

I stilled his hips as they thrust up to my mouth and slackened my jaw to take him deeper. A hand buried into my hair as he hit the back of my throat. Even then there was still a lot of flesh I couldn't fit, but I couldn't wait to try later. I twisted my head just as he twitched in my mouth before pulling my hair, forcing his cock free. He pulled my hair hard, arching me so my eyes were forced on his face. His expression tightened, and his lips parted as pleasure danced across his face.

After a few moments, his expression smoothed out and I heard a zip and the hard grip on my hair loosened.

Greyson scrubbed his face with a hand as he cursed. I grinned, happy with myself as I scooted the line of my body close to him. I made a point to graze the back of my index finger over his already hardening cock.

"Hurry up," I urged when the truck slowed. His hand flexed

on the wheel, and his jaw feathered. A strange look crossed his face, but he stepped on it.

The road wound between trees, going deeper into the countryside. It was maybe ten minutes later when we turned down a bumpy road, and I held on as the truck bounced on the uneven ground. The road cleared out to a big-ass three story house with southern-style architecture. The porch that wrapped around the first level was to die for.

"My goodness, your house is beautiful," I said, awed.

"Thanks," he muttered and once again scrubbed a hand over his smooth chin.

"Do you live here alone?"

"Yes," he answered after a beat of hesitation. Not much of a talker, huh? That was fine. I could help him out with that, although it wasn't like I needed him to talk for what I wanted to do to him.

The truck rumbled to a stop. He got out and came over to my side, holding out a hand to help me down. I jumped off, gripping his hand just to feel his touch. Greyson's grip flexed as he stepped through the door. The only sound was my boot heels clicking on the wood floors as he walked forward in the darkness.

I trailed my gaze over Greyson's stiff shoulders as he led me to a room. The curtains were opened, allowing me to see the tall king-size bed and the dark furnishings of the bedroom. Reaching up, I pressed my fingers into his shoulders. He stopped and let me massage him before I slid around, pushing him toward the wall until I was pressed against his hard chest.

Gripping his neck, I pulled him down.

A sound an awful lot like a growl burst from his mouth as he gripped my waist and trailed them to my ass. The stampeding went off in my stomach as he gripped me roughly and pressed me to him so his hard cock dug into my belly. Balancing with my hands on his shoulders, I jumped to wrap my legs around him.

Thank goodness for that farm work from living with my adoptive parents. It was the only reason I had the strength and balance to pull myself up.

A needy sigh escaped me when his dick pressed against my pussy. I needed him so badly. I moved my hips in a circular motion, grinding on him. My head tipped back at the tingles shooting through my body.

Greyson's lips slid over my neck, nipping and licking until he was at my mouth. It was pure skill the way he moved me without lifting his head.

Then the bed was under me, and I sank into the plush softness. Greyson kneeled at the edge of the mattress and dug his fingers into his dark hair. The lighting from the window was enough to let me see his shadowed green eyes.

"Fuck," he spat and raked his hand through his hair. I watched him from my place on the bed, about to push up and force him on top of me. Instead, he reached to the side and climbed me in a smooth motion. Greyson perched over me, regret flashing in his eyes before they steeled.

"What's going on?" Apprehension settled in my chest. It was that same feeling I got before I was dragged into Faerie.

"I wish you weren't what you are."

I couldn't get another word out because the next thing I knew, a rag settled over my nose and mouth.

My instincts kicked into overdrive. He wasn't fae. Right? No, his ears weren't like them. None of him pointed to being fae.

Camilla, now is not the time to mull!

I scrambled frantically, fear overpowering me. Tears sprung to my eyes as his grip tightened. No matter how hard I tried to get away, it was pointless. He wouldn't budge an inch. I used every muscle I'd built from horse riding and bucked like a mad bull. But it was no use.

I couldn't believe my goddamned luck. Dying of asphyxiation. The least he could have done was get me off before I died. The selfish, psychotic bastard.

CHAPTER 4
GREYSON

I watched her eyes slide close as the harsh thumping in my chest thundered in my ears. Camilla went limp, and I pulled away, trying to ignore the guilt eating my stomach. The door creaked behind me.

"It took you a while," Daniel said, amused. "I mean, I get why. She's delicious."

My hands fisted at my sides. I wanted to punch my closest friend in the face. I scowled and turned away from the still body on the bed and forced myself to ignore whatever the fuck was wrong with me. I was not in a place to question why I'd been a hair's breadth away from not using the chloroform-drenched hand towel Daniel had placed on the nightstand.

"Where are we putting her?" I gritted out between my clamped teeth.

"I put a pallet down in the cellar. I figured the cage we have for wolves would suit." Daniel moved to grab her, but I was quicker. I scooped her up, and she hung limply in my arms. My heart squeezed at how her head lulled to the side. She was such a lively little thing, and my chest ached at seeing her so out of it. Even though it was because of me.

I strode out with Daniel at my heels and headed to the kitchen, toward the basement door. The four locks lining the door frame were opened, and I slipped through. The mustiness of the moist room intensified with each step down the stairs.

The cage door was opened, and a hard pallet was on the ground with a folded blanket in the corner. I settled my burden with her head on the softness. Camilla's dark hair spread out, and as I moved away, I brushed my fingers over her smooth cheek.

I fisted my hand, realizing what I'd done, and grimaced. She looked so innocent with her lips slightly parted and her expression smoothed out with sleep. I jerked away. No fucking way would I be stupid enough to think a fae was good. I reached toward her back pocket and pulled her cell out before sliding it into my jeans.

I slammed the barred door closed and made sure the chains wound around it multiple times. These chains and bars would hold a werewolf, so it'd be more than enough for the slip of a girl. Forcing myself to turn away from the dank room, I was surprised to see Daniel waiting at the base of the stairs.

"Tristin called." Daniel held out the phone as I shoved past him. I thumbed the call back number, leaving Daniel to lock the door.

"I didn't expect you to call back so soon, Daniel," the alpha at the other end barked.

"You called?"

"Ah, Greyson. Daniel filled me in on what happened with the lead. You have one of the potential fae?"

"She reacted to wolfsbane unlike any human I'd ever seen. She has to be."

"Great, what are your plans?"

"Question her and see what she knows." My lips tightened in annoyance. The alpha in me hating being questioned. I was able to curb my instinct to growl and snap at Tristin.

"I've been talking to witches. There may be a way for us to get into Faerie. Would you be willing to hand her over?"

I forced my lips to remain shut when I sensed a denial forming. I scowled and paced the hallway. An odd energy worked its way through my limbs.

"When can you come get her?" I said instead of what I really wanted to say. Which teetered between *back the fuck off* and *mind your own fucking business.*

"In two weeks or so. I have to wait on the witches."

"Fine. I'll hold onto her and find out what she knows."

"Thank you, Greyson."

I grunted at the other alpha and hung up in a shittier mood than I'd been in before. Seconds later, I heard Daniel's soft steps as he came into the living room, where I ended up on the couch. I exhaled sharply before he spoke. "What did he say?"

"He's going to come for her. The witches may have a way to get into Faerie."

"We've been trying to find those portals for decades. This could be a breakthrough. We'd be able to cross over and get rid of the Queen once and for all." And that meant getting magic back and everything going back to how it was supposed to be.

"I know," I snapped and tilted my head to rest on the sofa.

"What are we going to do with her until they come?"

"Make sure she stays alive," I said, shrugging. "See what she knows."

"Tara will have a blast with that."

I tensed as something unfamiliar swirled in my chest. As if summoned, the door slammed open.

"I'm home," Tara called, strutting into the house like she owned the fucking place. She slid next to me on the couch and inched near my side. I tensed but forced myself to relax as she got closer. I was pure wolf, there was no separation of entities to distinguish the difference, so I should have wanted to sink into touch.

Touch went hand in hand with werewolves, but it'd never been something I was particularly fond of, especially when I shifted. I would say that was the only perk of magic being gone was I wasn't forced into shit I didn't want. Things that fell to me as alpha. The old ways had too many traditions that I was able to avoid without magic.

I tuned Daniel out as he caught her up on the situation.

"I'm going to introduce myself to the bitch," Tara said, her face twisting with vicious glee.

I gripped the back of her shirt as she stood to go. "No." I pushed a growl from my throat, so she understood I was serious. She huffed but angled her head in deference.

"She's passed out. It'd be worthless," Daniel explained, shooting me a confused look.

"I need to catch you up on the pack," Tara said. It seemed that the fae girl was too worthless to take up much of Tara's time. I refocused on what Tara was saying. The pack. Right. The people living on my land who depended on me. I snorted. It wasn't much of a pack anymore. Half of the homes on my property were empty when they used to be filled with werewolves. That seemed like so long ago. "Mrs. Jacobson is due to have her kid any day now. I went to check in with everyone."

"I'll make arrangements for medical care but ask her if she wants to be admitted to a hospital."

Tara nodded sagely, a smug smile to her lips. She'd been acting like my mate for the last century since she came looking for a safe place to stay. The situation, although unasked for, worked. She was conveniently there when I needed it. Her and the occasional one-night stand was enough to keep me satisfied.

That satisfaction wasn't remotely close to how hard I came earlier.

I'd never experienced the wrenching pleasure Camilla wrung from me and she'd only sucked me off. It was singlehandedly the sexiest thing I'd experienced in my long life. The sensations she drew from my dick were out of this fucking dimension. It had taken every bit of strength I had not to take her when I had her splayed before me. I shuddered at the memory, and Tara inched closer to my side.

"I'm going to hunt," Daniel said, smiling wolfishly. What he meant was he was going to go find some humans to fuck around with. It was the nightly routine he had going. He was lucky that matured Unnaturals couldn't get women pregnant, or he'd have been a father five hundred times over.

Tara's hand traced down my chest and fiddled with the edge of my jeans as she eyed my dick with a satisfied smile, thinking my hard on was for her. The last thing I would ever admit to anyone was that it was for a fae, so I didn't bother correcting her. Her lips trailed over my ears, and my eyes slid closed as I remembered Camilla's lips on mine. I found myself smiling, and I tensed. This was all wrong. Tara didn't bring the chaotic sensation to the forefront like Camilla did. Before I could push Tara away, a muffled bang sounded, almost too low for me to catch.

The basement.

I vaulted to my feet. Camilla was awake.

CHAPTER 5
CAMILLA

MY LASHES FELT LIKE THEY WEIGHED A THOUSAND pounds. I groaned and shook my head as I sat up. Memories rushed to the forefront as I registered the cage keeping me captive.

"No, no, no. Not again," I cried, getting to my feet. The room spun, and I swayed, gripping one of the bars. The metal was uncomfortable to touch. Like it had felt when I'd been shackled to iron chains in Faerie.

I yanked my hand away and whimpered. Panic pushed against my chest as I peered around. The only light in the room was a very thin slat on the upper side of the basement that filtered in a soft, pale glow from the moon.

The musty smell made my nose wrinkle, and I frantically took in the darkened area to see if I was alone. My shoulders slumped in relief and fear when I didn't make out others trapped with me. It was a good thing because my friends were safe, but . . . I was alone. I wracked my brain for explanations of why someone would capture me.

I clasped my hands together as they began to shake. Ever

since I'd escaped Faerie, confined places scared the bejesus out of me. Not just small places, but also dark ones. I tried to force my hands to stop their trembling. My fear went so deep, I couldn't even wrap myself under blankets anymore.

I crouched, looking to see if there was anything I could use as a weapon. Greyson was bound to come back eventually and damned if I'd just float about like a water lily. Who was he, anyway? What if it was like last time? I shivered at the thought of being a fae captive. The man didn't have the ears of a fae, but maybe he was a different type of Unnatural. Eliza and I had joked about what we'd do if we ever came across another, but the reality was not so great.

I stomped my foot in irritation when I found nothing and kicked the cot I'd woken from. The metal scraped across the ground, and I grinned evilly as I dipped to grab the edge.

Maybe I could break out before anyone came searching. With a firm grip, I grunted at the weight of the thing before I swung it against the bars. A loud ringing infiltrated the space and echoed off the walls as metal crashed on metal.

"Are you kiddin' me?" I yelled and kicked the bar as the cot fell to the side.

A door slammed opened, and light flooded the stairs, then the goddamned betrayer came into view. I settled my eyes on Greyson as he stormed down the steps. My lips twitched with disgust, and I curled my fingers to stifle the need to wrap them around his neck. Crossing my arms, I tucked my trembling hands in my armpits.

"You snake," I hissed. I couldn't see his face because of the way the shadows fell across what I now realize was a basement. "Why are you doing this? What have I ever done to you?"

A beat passed, and he surprised me by speaking. "Existed."

My jaw dropped at his audacity. This lily liver—

My eyes were drawn to a woman inches taller than me, her skin a few shades darker than my skin tone. She angled herself closer to Greyson, to his left but slightly behind him. Very obviously staking her claim. Irrational hurt filled me. He was not only a snake, but a tomcat. I refused to call him a dog. Dogs were loyal to the bone, and this man was nowhere close to that.

"Oh, is that how it is?" I stared her down. Who were these people? "Well, honey pie, did your boyfriend here tell you how I had him coming within seconds of putting him in my mouth?" My eyebrow flicked up. The girls would be so proud of me for not crumbling under pressure.

By the way she tensed, I could tell she wasn't happy about what I'd said, but a smug smile spread across her face. "Yet, you're behind bars, dumb fae."

I tried not to let off how disturbed I was. How did she know what I would be? She looked a couple of years older than me, but relatively normal.

"Where is the fae Queen?" Greyson asked in a low tone, nearing the cage.

Alarm strung through me. Goddammit, they *were* some type of creature. I took slow measured steps to the bars. We were a foot away with only metal separating us.

"What type of Unnaturals are y'all? Not fae, since you obviously have a thing against them. Vampires, maybe? I didn't feel fangs when we were making out. Greyson, honey, smile for me so I can double-check." It didn't occur to me that I should have acted clueless until rage flashed across his face.

Next thing I knew, my face was smacked against the cage. The sting of the bars hurt more than being kicked by a horse. I grunted and pressed my hand against my bleeding wound. I blinked through the pain.

"Don't speak to the alpha like that," the woman yelled. She'd moved really fast. Fast enough for me not to realize she'd gripped my shirt.

"Tara." A deep rumble broke out as I tried to staunch my nose bleed. "Out," Greyson ordered.

Alpha. I was dealing with goddamned werewolves.

I watched their shadows move away, my eyesight still not up to par. "I thought dogs were loyal," I called after them.

It wasn't until they disappeared that I let the tears that'd been building escape. I shook as I fell to the ground, trembling so hard it hurt.

CHAPTER 6
CAMILLA

IT WAS A GOOD THING I DIDN'T LIVE WITH MY parents. They'd be clucking about, worried I was out being a heathen. Sandy and Jarrod Richardson were old-fashioned, farm-owning country people. They'd adopted me when I was all of six years old. They'd given me a simple life and had supported my decisions—mostly.

They thought I was a little on the wild side, but they liked to say that was the Latina in my blood. I'd had multiple definitely-not-arguments with them about those ridiculous, problematic stereotypes, but they were the type to stick to their very narrow-minded views. If it weren't for Cosmo, my older brother, I would have gone crazy. Cosmo, the gentle giant who still lived with our parents to take care of the farm because Dad was getting too rickety for many of the jobs.

I was still working hard on trying to convince Cosmo to come live with me, but it had been a no-go so far. I just hope I survived so I could keep trying to convince him he didn't have to sacrifice his dreams to take care of the farm.

I may never get the chance to change his mind.

My shoulders slumped as the light from the thin slat brightened. It would be a while before Eliza or any of the other girls realized I was gone for longer than normal, but I hoped they didn't try looking for me. The last thing I wanted was them involved with werewolves.

By the look of things, it was dawn now, and I'd been unable to sleep the entire night. After Greyson and Tara's visit, I'd cried until I couldn't cry anymore.

The door sounded and I tensed, waiting with bated breath. What craziness awaited me now? I rolled my shoulders out and sat up in the middle of the cell, crossing my legs.

Light flooded the room when he flipped a switch, and it hurt my eyes until they adjusted. He was in a tight white shirt that left little to the imagination. On top of that, the jeans sheathing his lower half hugged him sensually. Why did he have to be so hot?

I narrowed my eyes at him as he grabbed a chair from the corner of the room and dragged it over to the middle of the basement. A sweating water bottle was placed at his feet. Until I spotted it, I didn't realize how thirsty I was. I licked my dry lips before looking away from his knowing gaze.

He sprawled in the chair with his legs spread wide. He didn't say anything, and I attempted to veil my increasing anxiety. "Tell me what you know about the Faerie Queen."

I focused on my nails, picking at them analytically. There was no way I'd tell him anything about any of my friends. No matter what.

"I wasn't expecting some grand romance. Just a good lay when I agreed to go home with you," I said conversationally.

"Can you sense portals to Faerie?" he asked in a bland tone.

"I mean, you were such a freaking amazing kisser. I was sure you knew how to use that mouth of yours." I sighed dramatically. "A shame you turned out to be a dirty snake." A growl sounded, rumbling like an engine. "Is that supposed to be threatening?" I threw my head back and laughed. "No, no, use that on *Tara*," I sneered. "She seems to respond to your orders, *Alpha*."

"Answer my fucking questions," he snarled, jerking to his feet. The chair fell on its back with his rough movement. My shoulders shook from laughter.

"Does the tantrum thing work?"

Greyson ran his hands through his hair. The dark strands ruffled with his jerky movements. He paced in front of the cage, and I set my chin in my hands and watched him. "You should give me my phone," I said casually.

He stopped and flicked an eyebrow up. "Do you mean this?"

He reached in his back pocket and pulled my cell out. The glittery case Eliza got me glinted in the light. My lips tightened at his smug expression.

"It was really surprising seeing that you didn't have a passcode." He flicked his finger up, and the screen illuminated. I knew what he stared down at. The screensaver was a picture of me and Eliza making a face at the camera. Eliza was right, not having a password came back to bite me on the ass.

"You can't keep me down here forever, you know. People will start asking questions."

"You did get a text from an Eliza . . ." Greyson paused, keeping me on edge.

"Let me text her back. She'll get the police involved if she thinks I'm in danger." I could send her the SOS. If one of us was ever in trouble, all we had to message each other was *I'm fine*. It was inconspicuous enough that we figured it could be used as the perfect code.

"Tara helped me with that." He held the chat box up to me, and the response to her was something I would say. *I'm doing exactly what you think I'm doing*. The bitch even included a wink emoji. I held back my frustrated yell. She probably searched for my most used emoji. Damn her intelligence.

"You're going to have to talk, or I'm going to have to pay a visit to your friend," he said, and it took everything in me not to react. Every single speck inside of me.

"And what are you going to do with her if she knows nothing?" I smirked and got to my feet, edging closer to the cage door. "You know it's a crime to kidnap people, right? Or is this a hobby?"

Greyson just smiled before he turned to go.

He was foolish if he thought I was going to talk. It wasn't like I knew the answer to his crazy questions anyway. The only thing I knew was Rae was working on freeing magic. But he didn't even deserve that response, and I'd never betray my friends.

CHAPTER 7
GREYSON

She still hadn't said anything, and I hadn't given her food or water in two days. I was about to break. I couldn't handle it anymore. Her face was drawn and exhausted, and every second I grew more concerned even though I was at fault.

I detested this weakness.

The first time I went down after Tara bashed her face into the bars, I had to force myself back from gathering her in my arms. Her nose seemed tender, and there were smears of leftover blood from the nosebleed. On top of that, her eyes were puffy and red.

It was obvious she'd been crying the entire night.

The bitterness when she spoke to me tore at my chest because it was at such odds with the playful spirit she'd shown me. I was a fucking mess. This desire for her was ridiculous. I'd experienced how traitorous fae were. The one and only time I'd been involved with one, I'd ended up getting my parents and brother murdered along with many pack members. I blamed it on maturing. When Unnaturals were first able to shift, they went through a stage where sex was craved to a painful extent, but I knew better than to have gotten involved with fucking fae.

If only the damn girl gave me answers, then I would make sure she had better accommodations. But she wouldn't talk. Daniel urged me to use more severe methods, but I put it off, even though I'd never before had qualms with torture.

I grabbed my tool bag and made my way to my truck. The Lourdes' windows needed to be fixed. The drive through my land was familiar and relaxing. I rolled the window down and enjoyed the fresh air brushing my face. It reminded me of a time when I ran through the forest on four paws at breakneck speed.

Putting the truck in park, I grabbed my bag and slammed the door. Cindy sped outside.

"Greyson!" she cried and clasped onto my legs with a giggle.

"Cindy Lou." I kneeled. "You're so tall. What are you, seven now?"

"No." She giggled. "I'm six still."

"My mistake," I said seriously and scooped her into my arms. She loved it when I made a big deal about her age. "Where's your mom?"

"Making Cory soup," she explained, suddenly sober. I tensed at the sadness in her voice, and my lips tightened. I knocked on the wooden door.

"Alpha Greyson," Ann Lourdes said as she stepped out, wiping her hands on her light blue apron.

"Hey, Ann." My smile faltered at the stress surrounding her eyes. I was failing my people. Weight settled on my shoulders. "Is it . . ."

"It's worse." Her expression crumpled, but she shot a look at Cindy in my arms, and her expression smoothed out. "Thank you for coming to fix his window. Lawrence is on his way back from his truck route, but it'll take him days."

"Anything for little Ann." She rolled her eyes. I'd known her since she was born, so it was hard to see her as anything older than the little girl in my arms. My aunt—my dad's sister—had been her great grandmother. My aunt hadn't reached maturity when magic was bound so she'd lived a human life on pack lands. Her descendants had followed in her footsteps, but when Ann started her family she'd moved away until her son became sick.

"Let's go work on that window." I kept hold of Cindy and swung my bag as I climbed the stairs to Cory's room. I pushed the door open. The sixteen-year-old boy was smaller than he should be. His skin was sallow, and he hunched into himself as if he was in pain. Lung cancer was sucking the life out of him. I swallowed hard when his eyes lit up.

"Greyson," he wheezed with a boyish grin.

"Hey, bud, heard your window isn't working."

"Yeah, it's a little cold." Cory peered over at the window and pulled the blanket tighter around him.

"Let's fix that." I perched Cindy at the edge of the bed. "Do you want to be my helper?"

She squealed, and Cory met my eyes, rolling them in a big brother fashion. Cindy had no idea what we were, what she would be if magic was ever freed, but Cory did, and that hope in his eyes every time he saw me gutted me.

If there was magic, he'd have his wolf's strength to fight off cancer.

Tomorrow I must try another way to get Camilla to talk. I had no other options.

CHAPTER 8
CAMILLA

IT WASN'T THE FIRST TIME I WENT WITHOUT FOOD for an extended period, especially considering I'd been kidnapped and held captive, but I'd forgotten how much it sucked. Scraping my messy hair back, I wished for a hairband to hold the mass away from my face. I was getting to a level of stank that rivaled the goats on Dad's farm.

If I could have anything right now, it'd be food, a toilette, a shower, and a nice plush bed. The goddamned low cot was awful for my back.

The door slammed open. It was like clockwork with Greyson's visits, but today he was early. I was positive it was going to go the same as every other time. He'd stride in, take a seat, and sit in a sprawled way that made my mouth water. Then, I'd piss him off until he left. It had become my little brand of entertainment.

The light came on, and a smug grin spread across my face as I plopped on my butt. He hated it when I grinned. I could tell when his jaw worked overtime.

When my eyes adjusted, my smile wilted. Tara smugly

sneered down at me with her hip cocked. She wore dark jeans and a lacy t-shirt I'd love to steal.

"I hear you're not talking for Greyson."

My head tilted back, and a loud guffaw passed my lips. "Bless your heart, and you think I'll talk to you?" I wiped imaginary tears from the corner of my eyes and tried not to smirk when her nose flared in irritation.

"You'll talk." A grin spread across her mouth. I hid the tremble of my hands by pressing them into the cold cement and leaning back. I was sure I was the vision of relaxation. "It's some archaic code he can't get out of his head since you're female."

The droll glance I shot her made her lips twitch. Oh, she was irritated.

With swift steps, Tara strode to the cage and unwound the chains. Hope sprung through me as the vision of escape filled my head. As soon as the door opened, I sprang to my feet. My legs burned with the sudden movement, but I pushed through and angled my shoulder out to bowl her over.

Before I could do anything, though, she gripped my hair, stopping me in my tracks, and effortlessly pulled me back. I fell to the ground in a heap.

"Did you forget I'm a werewolf?" Her eyebrow winged up, and she pushed me back with the bottom of her shoe when I tried to stand. Shit, I had. She seemed so human and not fae-like that I'd forgotten she was an immortal werewolf with extra strength.

"You're a smart doggy," I snapped. "You know, keeping someone hostage is a criminal offense. Be a *good girl,* and let me go."

Tara snorted in disgust before her leg flashed out, and she kicked my side. I grunted at the impact on my ribs and whimpered when the residual ache registered in my stunned brain.

"I'm holding back. That kick could have broken your rib, but I'm giving you a chance to talk. Keep testing me, fae." The tilt in her words was all attitude. The goddamned woman was sassing me as she kicked me. I gritted my teeth. "Tell me everything you know about Faerie and the Queen."

"This tenacity you have going on, is that how you managed to get Greyson? You know, desperation is just *ugly*," I tsked.

Rage flushed her face, and her dainty foot flew at me again. It hit me three times, and I heaved and jerked with each impact.

"Talk," she snapped. My lips tightened stubbornly. I could feel my body becoming a big bruise. Her next kick was aimed at my face. My head jerked to the side, and blood splattered across her jeans and specked the concrete.

"You stupid cow," I cried as my nose gushed blood. "Do your worst. I'm not talking."

She did do her worst. I lost count of how many times she struck me after the thirteenth. It was obvious she was making her way down my body with each question she asked.

Time blurred, and copper filled my nose, blotting out everything else. It was goddamned evil. That's what it was. She ensured my body ached with every movement I made, but at the same time, she was careful not to break anything.

"I heard about that human friend you live with. Does she know anything? Maybe I should question her."

"She doesn't know anything." I spat blood from my mouth and held back a gag. My chest constricted. Werewolves were just as bad as fae. I couldn't believe Greyson had allowed this after our teasing the last few days. Although, I shouldn't have been surprised since he was starving me. Bitterness rose, and for once,

I wished I was full fae so I could hold my own and beat every inch of *her* body.

"I think I'll go ask her." Tara's blurry form moved away, and I reached out and wrapped my hands around her ankles. Dammit, I needed to do something. I couldn't let Eliza get dragged here.

"I'll tell you everything I know. Leave her out of it. She's just a human," I lied. During one of our tiffs, Greyson disclosed to me that they had known I was going to be fae because I'd chugged down that drink they sent to our table the night at the bar. I would never give them more fodder by telling them that all the girls except one carried the fae gene. Thankfully, only Rae and I had chugged them down like they were ambrosia.

As Tara stopped and crossed her arms, I launched into how fae potentials like me came to be. "A fae King wanted to experiment with mates. He used some followers that hadn't closed the bond with their mate and got a witch to find a way to create one between the fae and human women just to see if they would create children. I didn't know what I was until almost a year ago when I was held captive in Faerie for months."

When I finished, Tara's eyebrows lowered as she contemplated me with narrowed eyes. "What do you know about the Queen?"

"Nothing." I forced a shrug even though it hurt like the dickens. "That's all the information I got before we managed to escape."

"You know," she began conversationally. "I'm not new to these methods of getting people to talk. Nor am I new to liars." A deep growl rumbled in her chest, and I swallowed hard, wanting to scoot away, but not having the strength. "You have the tendency to look to the left when you lie."

Tara swooped down and gripped my shirt with her super strength and pulled my face to her. "You're going to either tell me everything, or you're going to get better at lying."

"I don't know anything else," I screamed as she twisted my arm. That's when the pain became too much, and I passed out.

CHAPTER 9
GREYSON

"You need to seduce her." Daniel crunched into an apple.

"What?" I clenched the steering wheel as I pulled into my driveway.

"You heard me." Daniel drummed his fingers on his thigh. It was what he did when he was deep in thought. "Look, she's not talking, but you also refuse to go the torture route." With a shrug, he flicked the apple core out the window. "That leaves one option. Tell her some elaborate lie about needing her help to keep her here. And while we wait for Tristin to fetch her, seduce what she knows out of her."

"I've kept her locked in a basement and starved and you think she'll want to help me?"

"Greyson, you truly know nothing about women. Tell her about Cory and how you need her DNA for his cure and we're waiting for . . . a doctor, or whatever, to get here to test her blood. That way, she stays put until Tristin comes to get her for whatever lead he has with using her to get into Faerie, and you find out what she knows." A shit-eating grin spread across his face. "It's not a complete lie. She just won't know we're handing her over to someone in a few weeks."

I wanted to recoil from the idea but . . .

There would be no need to starve her. Her tired face and lackluster eyes flashed in my mind. I could give her a bedroom. It wasn't like she would be able to find her way out of here as long as I kept the car keys on me at all times.

Turning my truck off, I slid out. My feet quickly ate the distance to the house. Before Daniel brought up this plan, I figured I could try to bribe the damn girl, but his idea made more and more sense as I strode to the door.

I dropped the groceries on the kitchen island as a scream tore from below. I whirled to the door leading to the basement, not understanding why it was open. My shoes pounded against the wood stairs, and my nose prickled as the heavy scent of blood filled my nose. It took a moment for me to grasp the blood splattered on Tara's clothing and the limp, unconscious body at her feet curled into herself protectively. My gut twisted painfully as fear tightened my throat.

"Daniel was telling me how she wouldn't tell you anything, so I gave it a try. It took a while, and she's a shit-talker, but I finally got her to tell me about what she was." Tara's self-satisfied grin raised my metaphorical hackles, and I fisted my hand, fighting back the urge to tear out her throat.

Tara's eyes widened nervously. There was a loud engine rumbling in the room, and I realized I was growling. I needed to hold it together.

"Get out."

Tara didn't think to disobey. As soon as she sped out of the room, I ran to Camilla and fell to my knees beside her. Nausea crawled up my throat. I curled my arms under her, and she fell limply into my hold, a visceral pain slashing my chest. There were purple-and-black bruises gaining color on every inch of skin I could see. Blood dried on her face, crusted and beginning to flake.

I gently cuddled her to me and made my way to the upstairs empty bedroom. Fortunately, Tara and Daniel were gone. Kicking the bedroom door shut behind me, I set her on the mattress. The clothes she wore were dusty and bloody. When she woke up, I'd make sure she got a bath. That should help with the bruises, too.

Grabbing the folded blanket, I tucked it around her shoulders so she wouldn't be cold. I took a beat and inhaled sharply. What the fuck was I doing?

Shaking my head, I reasoned the gut-wrenching concern was purely fabricated. I needed her to think I cared what happened to her. This was just to gain her trust. It had to be.

I could have left to my bedroom, but my feet refused to move. Instead, I plopped into the chair in the corner and watched her chest rise and fall.

CHAPTER 10
CAMILLA

Blinking hurt. I wiggled into a soft bed and couldn't even enjoy it because I'd gotten the crap kicked out of me. I whimpered. Pain radiated through every inch of my body.

"Camilla." Greyson's low disembodied voice came from somewhere. My throat knotted, and I felt a shadow of pain when I popped from the bed. Edging back against the headboard, I held my trembling hands in front of me to ward him off.

Greyson's lips tightened, and he stepped away from me with his hands up. "I'm not going to hurt you."

"Aren't you a peach?" I sneered with false bravado. Clenching my hands, I set them down. A groan built in my chest at the tug at my sides. Greyson reached out again, and I mustered up enough energy to swat the paw away. Goddamn werewolf. I ached to be fae. During my captivity in Faerie, I'd witnessed how violent and strong they were. I wanted all that to show my *new* captors why they shouldn't have messed with me.

Though my temper had gotten out of hand a few times, I'd never been violent. I'd always preferred to lay on the honey while I subtly insulted someone. Now though? I wanted to be placed in a ring with Tara and Greyson. A sneer curled my lips at the thought of her. She deserved a good kicking.

Greyson was eerily still, but the flickering of his eyes indicated his frustration.

"Are you here to rub in what'll keep happening if I don't talk?" My hands fisted in the soft bedsheets. "Because you might as well kill me. I told your minion all I know."

The remnants of betrayal that he'd allowed my torture still stung. The emotion picked at the frayed edges of my will not to curl up and cry like a baby. I gripped the fresh wave of anger with both hands.

"Get out," I yelled and patted around me, wishing I had something hard to throw. I grabbed the first thing and chucked it. The rectangular pillow smacked him in the face and plopped on the ground. Stunned, he looked from me to the pillow. When the corner of his lip curled, the fury that receded turned into a tsunami.

Mustering strength I didn't know I had, I ignored the pinching pain in my side and grabbed the lamp on the nightstand. With a quick tug, the ceramic flew at his face.

I should have gone with the lamp first because he was ready this time, and he caught it before it shattered across his stupidly attractive face. With a growl, he twisted on his heels and slammed the door behind him.

Good riddance. I surveyed the barren room. The only furniture was the nightstand and the bed. Eyeing the window, I considered my avenues of escape. The wolves had extra senses, but if only I knew how far they ranged.

But before that . . . My bladder urged for release. Fortunately, there was a white door that complimented the eggshell coloring of the room. Once I took care of business and cleaned off the blood, I'd plan an escape.

I swayed when I pushed to my feet. The ache radiated to every inch of my flesh. It must have been the lack of food combined with pain because everything went dark as soon as I stepped forward.

I SANK DEEPER into the warmth, eyelids weighed down. I moaned at the comfort and the lap against my naked skin. I slid lower and water sloshed, sounding as if from far away. A hand pressed into my shoulder, staying me. I tensed. I was in a bathtub, and more importantly, I wasn't alone. My eyes flew open, and I gaped up at Greyson.

The tugging on my bruises exacerbated when I shot up and curled over my breasts. The rough material of my bra rasped across my arms, and I felt the constraint of panties. Relief loosened my shoulders as I met Greyson's shadowed gold and green eyes.

"Why am I in the bathtub?" I snapped defensively. A quick glance around confirmed that we were alone. I shrunk away from his touch, more from anger than fear.

An indent appeared between Greyson's eyebrows, and he moved his hands away. The lines around his lips tightened. "Relax," he ordered. "You fainted."

"And your answer was to strip me and put me in the bath? Are you trying to drown me?"

"You—" He cut off with a soft growl and tried to stifle the anger flashing across his eyes. "I wanted to clean the blood off you. It was the least I could do." He added the last part like it physically hurt for him to say the words.

I narrowed my eyes at him. "The least you could do is take me back to my home and leave me goddamned alone."

Greyson's nose flared, but he surprised me by not snapping even though that's exactly what it seemed he wanted to do. "I can't do that," he answered roughly. "I was going to invite you to eat lunch with me. I will explain everything then."

"Explain?" I scoffed. "It's a little too late to explain."

His jaw worked as he rubbed his neck. Tension lined his arm. I couldn't help the dip in my gaze as I watched the strength in the large bicep flex. Swallowing hard, I snapped out of my delirium and arranged my features into a nasty glare.

My body begged me for rest. The consistent ache in my limbs was a stark reminder of my beating, and most importantly, what he'd allowed. Betrayal rose like a tsunami.

"I didn't know what she was planning—"

"Don't lie to me," I yelled. Control rushed away from me as red filled my vision. I hated liars more than anything else in the world. Jaden had been a liar. The man I'd been in a relationship with had left me scarred. It was because of him that I did my best to stay away from burly sexy men like the one gnashing his teeth feet away from me. "You knew what your little girlfriend was going to do to me."

"She's not my anything, and I'm not a liar," he snapped. With a frustrated movement, he rubbed his hand across his chin. The scrape of whiskers rasped across his palm.

I eyed him disbelievingly. A sick part of me wiggled in excitement that he wasn't hers. The slope of his shoulders and the sincerity of his expression caused me to soften despite my resolve. He had no qualms before in treating me as he wanted.

What could possibly be the reason for this turn? Could he honestly be apologetic?

"I'm sorry she did this to you." He grazed one of the many bruises on my arm. I tensed as a rush of desire pierced me like a hot brand. I pulled away from his touch as quickly as he snatched his hand back. A scowl settled back on his face.

"Let's get you cleaned up," he said gruffly. He dipped a hand towel in a bowl of water at his feet that I hadn't noticed. The towel soaked the water up, and he squeezed to expel the excess. The cloth rubbed against my cheek gently. My shoulders were so tense, I felt ready to snap, but I was too stunned at the gentle ministrations to do anything about it.

I held my breath as he moved to my nose. The scent of copper intensified the more he brushed the fabric across my face. I winced as he touched a particular painful section on my cheek. Greyson's touch became gentler if that was possible.

I wasn't looking forward to seeing how messed up my face was. When he pulled it away, the entire rag was red. Probably as red as the blush on my face. What in the cow shit was going on with me? The last emotion I should be feeling was attraction for this . . . *wolf.*

I brushed my wet, tangled hair behind my ears. Greyson rinsed the rag in the bowl. Butterflies burst into my stomach when I realized he was going to go back to tending to me. I scrutinized the sudsy water. A layer of soap floated at the top. The blood could all be washed away with a quick dunk of my head, even if it stung the cuts on my face. But it was a risk I had to make. I needed to snap myself out of this lustful haze.

At Greyson's movement forward, I plunged my face in. I worked quickly before the pain set in, and with swift swipes, I scrubbed my face.

I pulled up from the water with a gasp. The sudsy droplets trailed down my face, and as the air hit my lungs, the stinging set in. I'd stepped in a fire ant hill once. The little stabbing prickles had spread across my foot and leg with a burning ache. It felt like that, but on my face.

Cursing, I fanned my face to stop the burn on my eyebrow, nose, and cheek, the places I was sure to see open cuts when I got in front of a mirror. I sputtered droplets from my mouth as the sting persisted.

"There's soap in there," Greyson snapped, and a fresh cotton towel settled across my cheeks and then over my forehead. He gripped the back of my neck and set the material on my face to dab the rest of the water away. I watched him with wide eyes.

Greyson's lips twisted, and I read the frustration in his gaze. I was at a complete loss for words. And that foreign sensation in my gut spread further. I clasped my hands beneath the water, digging my nails into my flesh as he finished.

"Where are my clothes?" I asked breathlessly.

"They were covered in blood. I put them to wash."

"I'm not hanging around like this." I waved a hand down my body. His eyes followed my movement and attached to the swell of my breast popping over my lavender bra. They were nothing to cry home about, but the bra was my special going-out bra, and it treated the girls right. "Eyes up here."

I gripped his chin and forced him to look at me. The stubble scraped my fingers, and I retracted as if I had been burned. My eyes dropped, but I quickly peeked back at him and glared. I was *not* feeling fluttery. I refused to feel fluttery. Greyson's eyes were just as shielded and defensive as mine when he pulled away. He jerked his chin to the side.

I followed the direction he gestured to a pile of clothing set on the edge of the counter. "You can leave now," I snapped without looking at him.

If my face was as hot as it felt, then it had to be as red as my mother's *Sunday's Best* lipstick. He growled, which I summarily ignored. He proved he didn't like that by growling again and slamming the door on his way out.

I sucked on my lower lip as I eyed the lip of the tub and the pristine white floors. Gripping the edge of the bath, I pulled myself up. My arms strained and trembled, but I managed to get to my knees. The aches were tough, but the tingling of my legs and the hunger twisting my stomach were worse.

Eyes fluttering, I sunk deep into the tub again. Goddammit. I balefully eyed the door the big brute had strode through and cursed under my breath.

"All right, I need help," I snapped, petulant.

The door opened seconds later, and his smug expression stared back at me. I wanted to flick the eyebrow he arched high. He gripped a big fluffy towel, and in a smooth motion, he gripped me under the arms and tugged me to stand. I swayed, but he somehow managed to keep me upright and maneuvered the towel over my shoulders. It tickled where droplets of water trickled down my leg.

I yelped as he swept me up, grabbing the clothing as he went. My stomach tightened at the easy way he handled me. I wasn't sure if it was the sheer size of him or the animalistic air he had about him, but I wanted him. The need was primitive and wild.

I gritted my teeth, angry with myself. What in the world was wrong with me? He'd not only tricked me, captured me, and starved me, but there had to be something up with his sudden turn in behavior.

"Why are you being nice all of the sudden?" Suspicion seeped from my voice. There was an ulterior motive here. I just needed to pinpoint it. Fortunately, the lights were on in the bedroom, so I was able to see the tick in his jaw as his answer.

He set me on the bed gently and then I was sputtering as he shoved a shirt over my head. I made an odd noise as I floundered.

"My bra is wet," I cried as he forced my arms through the shirt holes. "I can dress myself." I huffed but he ignored me.

"I figured you can wear this until I get you better fitting clothing."

I gaped down at the black shirt that dwarfed me. It was obviously his. Greyson reached out and tugged the collar back on my shoulder when it fell to the side and exposed my smooth, tan skin. A shadow passed over his face, and he agitatedly shoved his hand through his hair.

"Get under the covers," he ordered gruffly.

I scooted back until I could pull the covers over me and froze. Why was I listening to him? I scowled. It was ingrained in me to follow directions when said in a certain tone. Working on the farm with my father and brother, there had been no option other than listening. We had to work as a team, and I'd been at the bottom of the pecking order, which meant I had to be good at doing as I was told.

Maybe that was why I didn't follow directions in every other aspect of my life.

My nose wiggled as I scented chicken and forgot my ire. Hunger swept through me with a vengeance. Greyson sat at the edge of the bed and gripped a steaming bowl of soup that had been set on the nightstand. I blinked in utter shock at the way his hands engulfed the dish.

"Here," he said gruffly, and a spoon headed my way. Snapping out of it, I evaded the soup. A growl rumbled in the room, and I scowled at him. "You need to eat."

"Nope. You probably poisoned it."

"If I wanted to kill you, I would snap your neck." The words chilled me and in no way made me feel better. He sighed, exasperated. "I won't hurt you."

The spoon came at me again. I turned my head and pursed my lips stubbornly.

"Do you want to heal?" That rumble filled the room, and he placed the spoon in his mouth. "See, no poison." I twisted my head when it came at me again. "If you don't eat, I'm going to force you. You're so weak, you can hardly stand."

My lip curled up at the audacity. Were all werewolves such dicks? "I wouldn't be this weak if you hadn't starved me."

He grimaced, guilt straining his features, and bent his head, conceding the point. Hating that I had to take his help, I glared at him. This was a man I was attracted to and had seen in the throes of an orgasm. There was a joke there somewhere.

"I was desperate. I handled everything poorly." He placed the bowl in my lap, and I gripped it before it sloshed onto the bed. "When you've regained your strength, I'll explain everything. I hope you can understand my motives."

"No more cage?"

"No."

"Can I have my phone back?"

"We'll revisit it once you regain your strength." That was just a polite way of saying *no*.

The soup looked pretty good. Carrots and potatoes flowed

with pieces of chicken, and my stomach twisted with hunger. He had one thing right. I needed to regain my strength. Once I ate my food and rested properly, I was positive I would feel okay enough to escape. Giving in, I slipped the spoon in my mouth and almost melted with pleasure at the explosion of taste.

I wasn't sure if I fell asleep after the eighth or tenth bite, but the room faded away with Greyson sitting in the chair.

CHAPTER 11
GREYSON

THE BED CREAKED SLIGHTLY, AND I FORCED MY expression to remain smooth. My captive—Camilla—was trying to escape. I kept trying to force myself to think of her as a thing, as a filthy fae, but it was proving difficult.

The wing of her eyebrow that flicked up and the fire that lit up her eyes with indignation was *cute*. A word I never thought to attribute to a fae. I shouldn't have agreed to Daniel's foolhardy plan to seduce her to get information. I needed to focus on what mattered, but she roused my temper unlike anything I'd ever felt. I was unflappable. You had to be as the alpha of one of the strongest packs, or what used to be one of the strongest packs. Without our wolves, most who hadn't matured and those who no longer felt the need to be near a pack had left. Those that remained didn't feel my dominance at an instinctual level.

What was left at the forefront was our more human side even though the wolf tied within made us immortal and allowed enhancements. The heightened strength, speed, and sense of smell was nothing like having our full power and ability.

And all of this pain was caused by the fae.

A flash of anger speared my gut and settled with the bitterness that had simmered the last centuries. I clutched onto that resentment with both hands to remind myself of what was at stake. We'd never been so close to returning magic, and if we managed to find a way to Faerie where the Queen had run off to, then all this pain would be over. I wouldn't have to watch my people die human deaths or suffer from sickness.

That didn't fully explain what I was doing sitting in a chair as she slept. Nor did it explain helping her wash off. But when I'd heard the thump of her body hitting the floor, I hadn't been able to help myself. I pulled her into my arms, and the blood on her soft face had made my chest tightened. In the next moment, I was tugging her clothing off and setting her in the bath.

Frustration prickled at my neck. I was only keeping watch so she wouldn't try to escape. There was no other reason. Least of all worry that Tara would sneak in and continue her torture.

That was another pain in the ass I had to address. Hopefully, Daniel had told her to steer clear of me. Else I might actually kill her.

I'd never been an unfair alpha. I'd never tortured women. Even fae.

When Tara joined my pack a little more than a century ago, I'd not questioned her past even though I understood it was a bloody one. She'd been a female rogue.

And the little she had told me, she'd fallen in with a band of male rogues. A little makeshift pack without an actual alpha.

It was a recipe for disaster, but fortunately for them, they made it work. Alphas were vital to a pack, and they were there for order and protection. They kept wolves in line and strengthened the unit. If there wasn't one, wolves were volatile.

Although alphas were rare, packs were usually smaller, which made the pack I came from an outlier as well as one of the more powerful well-known ones before magic was bound. That was shy of three hundred years ago.

The soft hiss of the sheet sliding off her skin sounded, and as I'd been waiting for her to do, she settled her feet on the ground. The slight rasp of the carpet brushed across her bare skin as she inched to the door.

I couldn't wait to see how she managed to open the door without noise. I kept my eyes shut, regulating my breathing. If I truly had been sleeping, she could have easily escaped with how stealthy she was being.

A strange glee filled me. I wanted to chase her. I loved the way she challenged me, and that wasn't part of the plan. Least of all this insane desire to press my lips to hers.

When her shoulder had been bare, I'd thought back to the feeling of her luscious lips wrapped around my cock, and said cock had twitched. I wanted her there again. I wanted her. Period.

The door creaked, and I peeked to see her skulk out. I sprung to my feet, waiting long enough to hear the squeal of the floorboard near the door before I went to stop her.

A grin spread across my lips.

I'd experienced enough in my long life to know she'd try to escape as soon she could. The determination in her little body was too great for her not to.

But I was a born hunter. I could be silent. That's why she didn't hear me shadowing her as she made her way downstairs. She stuttered to a stop when she stepped on a particularly squeaky stair, and my lips twitched at how quickly she froze. I was sure she wanted to curse if the tightening of her fist on the rail was any indication. Soon, she mustered up enough gall to keep going.

Once she was at the base of the stairs, I decided to clue her in to my presence. I cleared my throat, and every inch of her went taut. Then she dashed down the hallway, toward the door. I gave chase, and like the sick fuck I was, I got hard from it.

All I wanted to do when I captured her was turn her around, spread her legs open, and bury my face in her pussy. I wanted to lick her and tease her until she clawed me. Until she let me fuck her so hard she forgot her very name. Or until I forgot what she was . . .

A burst of speed fueled me, and I gripped her by the waist as she touched the doorknob. Her bare feet swung wildly. It reminded me of capturing a cat by the scruff of its neck.

I pressed her front to the door so she wouldn't hurt herself by kicking me. All I succeeded in doing was pressing my cock against her ass. She froze and, in the next instant, arched, pushing against my length. A groan ripped from my chest, and I panted with need. She moaned in answer, and in a blink, she threw her elbow back into my stomach.

I dropped her from surprise, and she landed in an ungraceful pile on the floor. Camilla glared and sputtered dark hair from her mouth as she rubbed her elbow. Scowling right back, I crossed my arms so I wouldn't reach down and pick her up like I wanted to.

My loose shirt flitted to a standstill, emphasizing her curvy hips as her stomach growled. My scowl intensified.

"I'll make you breakfast." It had to be around six in the morning by this point, perhaps a little too early for breakfast, but she needed something more substantive in her system than soup. I watched her eye the door as I turned my back, expecting her to follow. "I'll force you to the table and tie you up."

She grumbled under her breath as I guided her to the kitchen. Camilla scowled at the door leading to the basement. The locks were all open, but the door was closed. She settled on the chair at the kitchen island farthest from that door.

Pulling out the fixings for omelets, I turned to the stove and flared it to life before deftly cutting up bacon and turkey and mixing it into a bowl.

I watched her as she silently eyed the furniture of the living room connected to the kitchen. I tried to see the rooms from new eyes—from her eyes.

The living room was large with a seventy-five-inch television hanging from the wall. A dark brown couch curved around the front of it with a coffee table scuffed with shoe marks in the middle of the area. The hardwood floor led all the way to through the kitchen. The same color was throughout the house. A dark brown. The island was pristine white and the only place to eat. Four tall chairs were tucked beneath the ledge, all except for the one Camilla sat in.

My house had zero touches of femininity. I wished I knew what Camilla was thinking as she gazed around. Her eyes settled on mine and slid down to the steaming pan on the stove. I jolted and shook my head slightly. Why was I woolgathering?

The pan sizzled, and I poured the egg mixture.

"I need to explain something." Really, I needed to lie to get her to trust me. Daniel's words played in my head. I needed to get her to stay long enough for Tristin to come get her.

My conscience twisted with denial. I ground my teeth. What was wrong with me? Maybe it was because I'd let her suck me off. Or it could be some sort of immortal midlife crisis catching up to me from all of the questionable shit I'd done in my life.

"And that is?" she said, impatiently waving her hand.

I turned back to the almost finished omelet as I answered, not wanting her to see the tightening of my face. "A packmate is dying."

"What does that have to do with me?"

I folded the eggs into an omelet shape before sliding it onto a plate. If I didn't already know I was going to hell for everything I'd ever done in my life, this would be the turning point. I was going to use Cory's sickness to trick her. "There's a . . . theory that your blood can be used to heal him because of what you are."

"Why would I help?" She sneered up at me as a strange expression flashed in her eyes that I couldn't read.

"He's just an innocent boy." Her shoulders tensed, and I pushed on. "He's been battling lung cancer for the last year. He's stage four and running out of time."

Her expression dropped, and genuine concern seeped into her eyes, surprising me. "Then take my blood, or I'll give you my number and you can call me whenever you need it, but you don't have to keep me prisoner."

Shit. I needed to lie better.

"It needs to be fresh." I slid the perfectly folded bacon and turkey omelet in front of her before pouring orange juice into a clear glass. The indent that appeared between her eyes indicated her skepticism. "We're waiting for a witch to visit in a few weeks. She may have found a temporary cure, but she needs fae blood to test it. I only have a split second of her time before she leaves. She's known for her fickleness."

"I'm not fae yet, though." Shit, there were too many holes.

I scratched my eyebrow, digging for more bullshit to spout. "No, but you have the gene, even though it's dormant." I let my desperation for Cory slip into my tone. "Just give me a chance before you decide. Let me introduce you to his family. You could be the reason they don't lose their son." I was such an ass, but I was backed into a corner.

It would save him, just not in the way she thought. If Tristin's witch friends were able to use her blood to get into Faerie, we'd be able to kill the Queen and free magic. From there, all magic would be freed and then I could begin the search of getting Cory a magical cure. Or at least something to keep him alive until he reached maturity at twenty-two.

Before reaching maturity, all Unnaturals were vulnerable, but all you needed to do was survive until then. Once that happened, the change would occur, and human sickness wouldn't be able to touch him.

It was all smoke and mirrors, but it was the only chance to get magic back.

Camilla turned pensive, and the warring decision played out in her eyes. What was going through her mind? I could read nothing substantive in her shuttered gaze.

"What if I don't agree? Are you keeping me here?"

"I don't want to force you . . ."

I didn't give her a direct answer because the truth was, I had to keep her here even if I said she wasn't my prisoner. That was exactly what she was. I'd prefer it if I didn't have to keep her locked in the basement for however long, but she was vital to helping the pack, and I wouldn't let the ones relying on me down again.

She gazed at me sardonically, then a sly smile spread across her lips. "I figure you'll lock me in that dank room downstairs if I don't agree, so you know what? I agree."

Shit. I was going to need to be on her ass the entire time I had her here. The hellion would try to escape again. I had no doubt about it.

CHAPTER 12
CAMILLA

IT WAS MY ONLY CHOICE AS I SAW IT. I WASN'T ABOUT to say no and chance him locking me up again. I'd had enough of that, thank you kindly. I guess this was what he'd meant when he said he wouldn't put me in the cage anymore. He was just switching it out for a bigger, more elaborate cage. Because jeez, the house was huge. I'd almost lost my way when I'd stepped out of that room upstairs and attempted my first escape.

That's exactly what it was. My *first* attempt. If I wasn't locked in that dank room, I actually got a shot of learning my surroundings and snooping. Maybe if I could figure out where the car keys were, I'd have a better chance.

And yet there was a boy dying from cancer. I wanted to help him for no other reason than it was the right thing to do. When Greyson mentioned the family, a knife had twisted in my stomach, and I thought of Cosmo ever being in that situation. It got more real. I didn't want to meet the family because once I did, there would be no turning back. I would undoubtedly stay and wait for this witch who could potentially use my blood to heal the boy.

I chugged the orange juice down and noticed I'd devoured the omelet as he'd talked. I had hardly tasted it because I was so hungry, but it sat pleasantly in my stomach. The full sensation relaxed me more than I thought possible.

I flicked a look at him as he scooped up the plate and set it in the sink. My stomach flipped again. I'd never had a man feed me, let alone make me breakfast, and the effect was sexy. His shirt stretched across his shoulders, and my mouth watered for something other than food. I imagined my nails digging into the hard muscle.

I wiggled in the tall bar chair I sat on and smoothed down his shirt that fit me like a dress. Thankfully, my underthings had dried throughout the night, but it was any wonder I'd been able to sleep in them.

"Go get dressed, I'll take you over to visit."

The order made my spine straighten painfully, and I glared at him. This alpha business wasn't going to work with me. I opened my lips in preparation for a rant just as the door slammed open from the hall.

I jumped to my feet. My hands fisted, and I prepared myself for the woman who beat the crap out of me to come in. Now that I felt a little better, I'd go down swinging if she tried anything.

I stepped into the hallway as a little bundle crashed into my legs, sobbing. When a hand hit my leg, a bruise pulsed in answer. I gawked down. What the hell?

"W-where—" She began crying harder. I let out a shuddered breath. Was this Greyson's kid? I eyed her closer. The clothing she wore was dirty and caked in mud.

"Greyson," I called, freaking out a little. My wide eyes turned to him on the other side of the island.

"Cindy Lou," he barked, and his swift strides reached us in seconds. The little girl let me go and barreled into him. The large gruff man who drove me absolutely crazy knelt and opened his arms for her. Concern lined his face.

"What are you doing here?" He angled her back and took in her disheveled little clothes. "Did you run here?" The stunned way he said it gave me the impression that her house wasn't close.

"My mom won't wake up," she said between hiccups. My heart twisted for the kid who had to be anything from six to eight.

He swept her up and strode toward the hallway.

"Let's go," he snapped at me.

"I need clothes!" I waved a hand down at my inappropriate attire. He grabbed a large corduroyed coat from the closet and shoved it at me. I slid my arms through and zipped it. The coarse material brushed my knees. I pulled my hair out and moved to run upstairs to get my boots tucked by the bed.

"No time," he said in a clipped tone and waved to the male work boots sitting by the door. I offered him a baleful glare as I slipped them on. The shoes engulfed me. I'd never thought I'd rue the fact that I walked around indoors barefoot.

Greyson whipped the door open and strode to the gravel driveway where his truck was parked. I clopped up to the car like an awkward calf in the too-big shoes. These were definitely his, and just like everything else I had on that was his, it didn't fit at all.

I tripped and fell into the gravel. My knee stung as jagged rocks tore open the flesh.

Greyson was suddenly beside me, growling. He easily lifted me in his arms, deposited me in the back seat. I gawked as he handled me with care, and I looked over at Cindy situated next to me. Her eyes swam with tears.

I wrapped my arm around her on instinct. Greyson tensed above me, hovering as he'd clicked in the buckle to my seatbelt. If I inched up, my lips would graze his jaw.

My heart fluttered with the need to do exactly that, but he jerked back in the next instant and slammed into the front seat. Seconds later, the tires spun and gravel spit as he took off at breakneck speed. I gripped Cindy harder, and she hesitantly got closer to me.

"Hey, I'm Camilla, but you can call me Cam." I tried to smile comfortingly, but I was worried about the utter fear in her eyes.

"Hi," she said, dropping her gaze.

"We'll get to your mom quickly, okay? Don't be too worried. I'm sure Greyson will help her however she needs."

Cindy's lower lip trembled, and my heart clenched for her. Poor girl. The last thing she needed to worry about was her mom. She should be running wild, not running through the forest to get help because her mom collapsed.

I gripped her harder as the truck bounced through an uneven pathway. I could see Greyson's tight expression through the visor, surprised he'd angled the mirror to look at the back. I wondered if it was because he didn't trust me. I offered a glare and smoothed Cindy's hair down.

I wasn't down for being a prisoner, but I wasn't a monster. He nodded slightly. I wasn't sure if he'd read the message through my eyes or what, but the tightness around his softened, and the gold flecks seemed to churn with warmth. He had such a unique eye color that often seemed less green and more golden. My belly twisted in answer. I licked my lips and turned away, suddenly nervous.

Why was he making me react this way? I needed to get a hold of myself. This was getting out of hand. He'd practically admitted that he'd keep me prisoner no matter what.

Cindy distracted me by roughly rubbing her eyes. The truck jostled again and skidded to a stop in front of a two-story house.

"Go ahead, I'll bring Cindy inside," I said quickly. Greyson shot me a glance through the mirror before pushing the door open and disappearing.

I unbuckled Cindy and myself before opening the door. As I moved back, I saw the truck keys hanging in the ignition. I tensed and, for a split second, debated about getting out of here.

Cindy's sniffle distracted me, and I slumped, discarding the idea. I gripped the keys, turning off the ignition, and slipped them in my pocket before gripping Cindy under her legs and hoisting her up.

I wasn't terribly tall, so it took some adjusting to get her comfortably in my arms. She wrapped her arms around my neck. Slowly, I made my way to the open front door. I was glad the pathway was paved with flat cement blocks. It made my awkward shuffling in the overly large work boots easier to manage.

I climbed up the steps, huffing a little under the strain, and was finally inside the house. I took in the flowery wallpaper adorning the entrance hallway. "Where did your mom fall, Cindy girl?"

She removed one of her thin arms from my neck and wobblily pointed. I followed her direction and stepped into the kitchen.

Greyson was checking a woman's head as he forced her to drink water. My eyes met the surprised blue eyes of a brunette woman. She was probably in her thirties if I were to guess. She seemed to be close to Greyson's age, even though he was immortal as a werewolf.

Her eyes tightened. Despite the suspicion, my momma raised me right, so I offered her a smile. "Are you okay?"

Her eyebrow twitched when I spoke. It was probably because of my thick southern accent. Stereotypically speaking, I didn't sound like what many people thought I would sound like, which was something I'd heard multiple times in my life.

"Who is this, Greyson?" the woman asked, giving me the evil eye.

Who was she to Greyson? And why did the thought of her being close to him sting so badly? I tensed at the sharp words.

"My name is Camilla, ma'am," I responded sweetly, when I wanted to do the exact opposite. I tacked on the *ma'am* pettily. More like bitc—

"Ann Lourdes," she responded tightly.

"Mommy." Cindy's voice warbled. Ann smiled, eyeing me wearily, so I offered a slight smile.

"Come here, Cindy," Ann said in a calm tone, as if I were a bear that would attack if she didn't get her child out of my arms.

I quickly set her down and took a step away from them. My eyes flashed to Greyson and saw the warmth I'd never seen directed at me, and my stomach churned. It was obvious he cared about her, but what kind was it? The tightness in my chest heightened, and I inhaled sharply. Why was I so jostled by the possibility that he was in love with someone?

"I'm okay," Ann said with a squeeze to her daughter's

hand. My own heart warmed at the sight of mother and daughter. An ache to see my own mom filled me. "It must be the stress." Ann waved away Greyson as he tried to pick her up.

There was a crash from upstairs, and everyone tensed. Ann tried to push to her feet.

"Don't get up," he snapped. Greyson peered up at me, and there was almost an apologetic look in his eyes. "Can you go check on Cory?"

My heart stuttered painfully as I watched him handle her gently. With tight lips, I nodded. I figured that noise was Cory, and I clopped my way up the steps.

A thin, wiry boy leaned against the bed. His skin was sallow and his eyes tired. His harsh breathing quickened when I stepped through his open door.

"Hi, I'm Greyson's . . . friend, Cam." I lowered my voice, and he automatically relaxed.

"I fell," he said, face twisting. "I heard Cindy yelling and tried to go see what was wrong, but I must have passed out."

"Everything's fine. Your mom had a little accident, but Greyson is taking care of her." He nodded frantically, his youthful features pinched. "Is it okay if I sit here?" I asked, wanting to offer him help, but I could tell by the tension that he was confused.

"Yes," he stuttered, and his eyes slid closed. He had the lanky build of a teenager, but he seemed so weak. His bald head bent forward. I heard a sniffle, and my heart went out to him. I gingerly sat next to him.

"None of that," I muttered and set my hand on his shoulder. When he didn't shrug me off, I let my arm slide over his shoulders. Cory surprised me by turning into my hug and letting out a sob. I ran my hand down his back. He was still bigger than me despite his weak frame.

"I'm sorry. I don't cry. I don't know why I'm crying," he said with a shudder.

"It's okay. Sometimes it's easier to cry around strangers if we don't want to worry our loved ones. My momma says human nature is unexpected, and we often allow ourselves to be vulnerable around those we don't know. There's a reason people talk to bartenders." I cleared my throat, still soothing his back. "What I'm trying to say is you can let it out and I won't judge you."

"I don't want to worry my mom anymore. I wish I would just die."

My heart fell to my stomach at this young boy's pain. I swallowed hard to get rid of the knot that had formed in my throat. This was the boy Greyson needed me to heal. The one my blood would help.

In a split second, it was decided. I was going to help Cory however I could. Resolve filled me. The only type of resolve I ever felt for my brother, Cosmo.

"I can't tell you details, but Greyson is working to heal you. Don't give up. I promise I'll help however I can." Cory sobbed harder and squeezed me. "And I'll let you in on another little secret." He took a deep breath and pulled back a little. "My friend is the Queen of Faerie and she's working hard to unbind magic. Just keep your chin up and keep fighting. We just need you to get to maturity. Not too long, right?"

"I'm sixteen," he responded in a low tone, hope springing to life in his eyes.

"See, only a few years to go."

He nodded and pulled back and tilted his head against the

bed. I patted his hand. "Thank you," he said with his eyes squeezed closed.

"Anytime."

He hesitated but finally got around to what he wanted to ask. "What happened to your face?"

"I had a run-in with a door," I joked, and his laugh had an almost surprised edge to it.

I met Greyson's eyes as he came into the room with eerily silent steps. He took in Cory's slumped form, and worry filled his intense eyes. His hands clenched at his sides as he drank me in. I did the same to him, and the fluttering returned to the pit of my stomach.

"Are you okay, Cory?" he asked without moving his eyes from mine.

"Yes." Cory cleared his throat and wiped the remnant tears from his face. His shoulders straightened, and his expression changed. It was obvious he was trying to hide his vulnerability in front of Greyson. "Is my mom okay?"

"The stress got to her, but she'll be fine." Greyson surprised me by reaching down a hand. I slid my smaller one into his, and he helped me to my feet. He tugged a little too hard, though, and I bounced off his chest. I winced when the aches in my body made themselves known.

A stream of air huffed from my lips when his hand settled on my waist to steady me. Even under the thick coat, his touch scorched me. I followed Greyson's gaze to the cell phone next to Cory's bed.

"Next time, call me instead of trying to run out of here," he said gruffly.

Cory's head dipped with shame. I angled my arm and

elbowed his side. Giving him a warning look, I ignored how the shock on his face quickly morphed into a scowl.

Greyson cleared his throat and ran his hand over his chin. "Before we leave, I'm helping you get downstairs."

Cory nodded at Greyson, but I sensed his caution, so I rushed forward and out of the unbalancing proximity of Greyson. I held a hand down to Cory and braced myself when he took it. I settled his arm around my shoulders, and he leaned most of his weight on me. I used that hay-bale-throwing strength I'd built to keep us upright. We slowly made our way out of the room with Greyson hovering behind us.

"Where's the living room?" I muttered under my breath, and Cory came to my rescue by tilting his head in its direction. I almost stumbled because of the shoes, but Greyson's grip slid around my waist and kept me balanced. He left his touch there to wreak havoc on my insides.

The living room walls had the same floral pattern, and the couches were tan and large. Ann sat on one, sipping water, but she tensed when she saw me come in with her son. Her eyes dropped to Greyson's hand gripping my waist. I didn't give in to the urge to scowl at her and instead guided Cory to the other couch. Once he was safely seated, he let out a deep breath and relaxed.

I stepped back to Greyson's side, and he caught my arm when I tripped on the rug. I muttered my thanks as he released me. "It's the shoes. I'm not normally this clumsy."

His eyebrow flicked up, and he hummed. I narrowed my eyes at him and waved at the little family gathered.

"I'd like to come visit you if you don't mind," I said, looking at Cory.

His smile brightened, and he nodded vigorously. I was glad

the earlier defeat was gone from his expression. I nodded tightly at a stiff Ann and smiled at Cindy before turning and striding toward the front door. Greyson said something to Ann, but the words were too low for me to hear.

As I approached the truck, Greyson appeared next to me and froze by the driver's side. "Where are my keys?" he growled and narrowed suspicious eyes at me.

"Oh," I mumbled and fished in my pocket. When I jingled them in front of his face, he hesitated and reached for them. His hand brushed across mine, and we stood frozen, gazing at each other.

Butterflies fluttered through my stomach. I quickly turned and slid into the backseat, ignoring the tremble of my hands as I buckled in. I tried not to look up, but I was unable to resist.

Our eyes met in the mirror again, his eyebrows furrowed. "Do you understand now?"

I nodded tightly and forced myself to look away. "I understand, and I'll stay put."

CHAPTER 13
GREYSON

I PACED THE KITCHEN, THE WEIGHT OF CAMILLA'S cell phone heavy in my pocket. I couldn't believe I was debating returning it. And Daniel was still gone so he couldn't talk me out of the idea.

She'd handled Cindy and Cory with care. The gentle way she'd calmed them—she was a natural with kids. Then the way she hadn't taken off when I'd stupidly left the keys in the car.

I rubbed the back of my neck. "Fuck."

I was going to do it. Guilt festered in my gut at the building lies. The idea of giving her the phone only barely alleviated the stress in my stomach. I strode toward the room upstairs. I eyed the bedroom next to the one she stayed in and pushed it open.

I'd never invited Tara to stay with me, but I hadn't told her to leave either. Having her close was nothing but a convenience, and I never thought much about it. I stepped over a pile of clothing strewn across the floor. Tara was a messy person and had been since day one.

I'd made it clear that I would visit her when I wanted release, so this was the only room I'd ever fucked her in. I liked my own space, and it would be a cold day in hell before I allowed anyone in my bed. I didn't like my scent mingling with another. It was also the farthest from Daniel's room, and I'd had enough of Daniel and Tara's bickering, so the goal had been to keep them away from each other.

I pulled open all of Tara's drawers, having no idea where she kept things. I reached for two button-down shirts and two pairs of jeans. I exited the room to Camilla's door and slammed my fist on the door with more force than I meant to.

"Come in," she called from the other side.

I stepped through and was surprised to see her sitting on the edge of the bed with her eyes downcast. I automatically wanted to wrap her in my arms and ask her why she seemed so melancholic, but instead, I held out the clothing.

She gripped it mechanically and met my eyes. The wetness startled me. She'd been crying.

I floundered for words. Clearing my throat, I shuffled from foot to foot. "Are you okay?"

I internally cringed at the gruff edge to my words. I had zero speaking skills. I left the verbal seducing to Daniel. I was too old and too tired to play flirtatious games. Women always came to me anyway, so there was no need to use pretty words to get them to screw.

"You care about fae all of the sudden?" She snorted and hugged the clothes to her chest. "Whose are these anyway?"

"They were left by a . . . packmate." I struggled to get the sentence out and scowled. Why had I said that? For some reason, I didn't want her to know Tara lived here. I knew how that would sound. Like I was Tara's. That was the furthest thing we were to each other, despite Tara trying to fill the role of my mate without a bond.

She helped out when I was busy, and I never dissuaded her. That was my fault. I was confused by how uncomfortable I felt disclosing the living situation to the brown-haired beauty staring me down.

"Is your pack big?" Curiosity replaced the sadness in her eyes, and I found myself answering without thinking.

"Not anymore." I frowned, and her eyebrow arched. "Everything changed when magic was bound centuries ago."

She nodded slowly.

"And time moves differently in Faerie."

She *did* know something. Camilla tensed. I narrowed my eyes, but I let the comment go even though I wanted to force every facet of information from her plush lips.

"How did magic being bound change your pack?" she asked. The words spilled from her mouth one after the other, her accent thickening. A tell.

She was nervous. And fuck if it didn't make her even more adorable. I forced my thoughts away from this dangerous path.

"My pack pretty much disbanded. With magic bound, our wolf form became stuck within ourselves," I said with disgust, trying to assuage the guilt eating my insides. Sighing, I sat next to her. "The need for community and hierarchy the wolf craves vanished. It started small. With older wolves deciding to take off and become rogues. Then those that never matured into their wolves and didn't turn. Many of those decided to leave and live their lives as humans."

I went silent as I thought of the droves of Unnaturals who were supposed to turn wolf but never got the chance. I'd tried to keep track of some of those who had left, but soon they died, leaving behind their children.

"Their descendents are like me then." The tone was

contemplative, and I whipped my head in her direction. Camilla met my eyes, and her lips pressed together. "I guess there's no harm mentioning it," she murmured.

I swayed forward, filled with the need to coax her pink lips apart and curl my tongue against hers. I was the worst type of mutt. I wanted her—no, I hungered for her.

A scowl twisted my face, and her eyes tightened. She'd misunderstood the frustration on my face, but I couldn't afford to correct her, even as much as I wanted to.

"I told that woman about how the Faerie King decided to experiment with matings," she said, and I inclined my head hesitantly. "Well, there was a handful of fae that got humans pregnant. Those that were born with the gene are like other Unnaturals, weak and human-like until maturity. Then magic was bound, and the gene was passed on. That's how I'll be fae if Rae—" Her teeth clicked as she snapped her mouth shut.

"What?"

"What I was saying was that like you wolves that didn't mature, those with the fae gene didn't either but it passed on the gene." The confirmation she was keeping something hidden whipped my libido back into place. My jaw worked in an effort not to snap in anger. "If your pack is smaller, how big did it used to be?" she continued, attempting to change the conversation.

"Only around ten families live on the lands. I take care of them. I went from one hundred and fifty packmates to twenty." Big by pack standards, especially since packs tended to be smaller units, especially now. Perhaps they wouldn't have left so easily if I hadn't been such an irresponsible shit. Father had always been on my ass about my careless attitude. I hadn't listened until it was too late.

Hate bubbled in my chest, both for myself and the fae who had murdered a handful of my pack. If only I hadn't allowed *her* to come here.

"I'm sorry." A delicate, tan hand settled over mine, and every atom in my body perked up in attention. I shrugged, trying for nonchalance, but it was the furthest thing I felt.

Her hand tensed on mine. "You and Ann seemed close."

"We are." It was hard not to be close to Ann. It was interesting how she'd gone from looking up to me to trying to mother me. I could see the jealousy in Camilla's eyes, and I was absurdly pleased. She licked her lower lip, and I found my torso curving toward her.

Her breaths puffed against my lips as I neared. Despite my best judgment, I pressed my lips to hers and slipped my tongue into her mouth as I'd wanted to this entire time.

Camilla tensed for a split second before she kissed me back, her body melting into mine. A whimper escaped those precious lips, and that broke what little restraint I had left. I gripped her thigh and tugged her on top of me.

I needed her hot pussy. I needed to fuck her.

Her generous hips undulated on top of me, and a noise I'd never made before ripped from my chest. That felt amazing. Better than amazing.

Her small hands cupped my face, and I placed mine over them as she took control. Nipping her lip, I kissed my way to her neck and scraped my teeth over the sensitive flesh. What the fuck was wrong with me? I never put my teeth near anyone's neck. No wolf did. My shock melted away when Camilla palmed my dick over my jeans.

In a smooth motion, pinned her to the bed with my hips.

Without any hesitation, she wrapped her legs around my waist, the movement pressing me into her hot core.

"God, Boots," I muttered the endearment I'd wanted to call her since I'd seen her strutting around in those cowgirl boots. I slid the zipper of her borrowed coat down slowly. A possessive madness gripped me when my shirt was unveiled underneath. My chest rumbled. I gripped the loose collar and tugged it to the side, and then her covered breasts were in unveiled. Salivating at the sight of the swells, I tugged the lacy material down.

Her perfect brown nipples were pebbled, and I covered them with my mouth. I laved her breasts with attention, adoring the mewling noises spilling from her lips.

Adored.

What. The. Fuck. I didn't adore *anything*. I stiffened as Camilla wiggled downward, and her nipple popped out of my mouth.

"Grey. Greyson," Camilla moaned against the underside of my chin and deftly unbuttoned my jeans without looking. Anger filled me at the easy way she did it. The thought of her past sexual exploits jolted me enough to jerk me out of the lust-induced haze.

"Fuck," I yelled and fisted the blanket by her hair. Her hands froze at my waist as I tried to regain my senses. Her unfocused eyes blinked up at me, and my chest clenched with the need to slide down and tongue her heated pussy.

That fucking fae bitch flashed through my memory, and I tensed. I shouldn't be doing this. I wasn't going to get more wolves under my protection killed. My stupid decision had led to the destruction of my family. I pulled away even as my body urged me to sink into her.

"G-Greyson?"

I hated the way my heart squeezed at her uncertainty. I fisted my hands and pushed off the bed. I focused over her shoulder when I spoke, refusing to look at her. "This won't happen, fae," I spat.

She jerked back. I was such a fucking dick. I wanted to fall to my knees and explain. I was damaged. I needed to keep my priorities straight, and she was a reminder of all my failures. But I didn't say or do any of that.

"Your prejudices are noted," she replied crisply. I allowed myself to peek at her as she pulled herself together, her expression unreadable.

Tension hardened my shoulders. More than anything I wanted to run on all fours. The need to escape washed over me, and I fished for her phone in my pocket. I set it on the nightstand because I couldn't bring myself to touch her—I'd give in. I twisted toward the door with her hurt eyes following me.

Maybe I should fuck Tara, but even the thought deflated my stiff cock. I didn't want Tara. I wanted Boots. The woman I'd repeatedly lied to.

CHAPTER 14
CAMILLA

I gazed at the cell in one hand and touched my lips with the other. I was a goddamned hussy. That's what Eliza would call me. She'd be appalled at me, or well, she would be after high-fiving me.

Grimacing, I powered on my phone and saw a slew of texts from Eliza, Thea, and Rosalind. The first messages were all just checking in on me the night of the bar. It had been almost three days ago. I couldn't believe it. When I hadn't responded, their texts began to threaten getting the cops involved. Then that bitch had messaged Eliza as me, and the messages had stopped.

I opened a group chat and messaged them all that I was okay. I debated messaging them an SOS but quickly discarded the idea. I didn't want to put them on Greyson's radar. Instead, I sent the emojis of a cow, a girl, and an eggplant.

Eliza's response came back in the next second. *Yes, girl, ride him like a cowgirl!*

I rolled my eyes at my screen and cheesed so hard. I missed my bestie. I replied that they wouldn't hear back from me for a while and placed my phone on the nightstand.

Eliza and I had something extra special, but the bond the girls and I had forged by being kidnapped by the same psychos tied us together. Even Selena and Jasmine, who'd left. Our monthly check-in was coming up, though. Maybe this time I could convince everyone to meet up.

I'd invited everyone to live with me. Everyone but Jasmine, Selena, and obviously Rae had taken me up on my offer. Rae because she pretty much had to save the Unnatural world by finding a way to free magic. My poor friend was struggling with it, especially considering who her mate was.

I couldn't believe I'd almost mentioned Rae to Greyson. Yeah, Rae was Queen, but the way he spoke about fae didn't give me the confidence to tell him anything. Even if it *was* Rae who was working to free magic. Hopefully, it would be soon, then there'd be no worry about Cory getting healed. There had to be a way in the Unnatural world.

If this was all resolved quickly, I'd be able to go back to my life and leave behind the gruff werewolf.

I couldn't be stupid about him anymore, but he was hard to resist. His proximity got me going. When his muscular thigh pressed close to me, I'd had zero strength to refuse him.

It may have also been the way he'd been with Cindy and Cory. It was evident he loved them and vice versa. Although, I was a little skeptical about the exact relationship between him and Ann. He wouldn't have kissed me if they were a thing, right? Especially if there were kids involved.

Everything I'd seen of him so far told me he was different than Jaden. When I was around him, I was simultaneously comforted and aroused. I never felt relaxed around Jaden.

I shook off those Jaden thoughts and grabbed the clothing to take a quick shower. Looked like I was going commando.

I WRUNG my hair out with the towel. The shower had been exactly what I needed. The shirt fit fine, but the jeans were tight. I squatted a few times to loosen the fit as I finished with my hair.

As I took in the room, I debated what to do. My eyes flashed to the door. I was too energetic to sleep, not that I'd ever been a nap type person. Anyway, deciding that I would stay of my own volition should make it so I could explore the house, right?

Decided, I strode from the room. The clatter of plates sounded as I approached the staircase. Goddammit, I hoped that vicious bitch wasn't down there. I debated going back to my room but quickly nixed the idea. I quickened my pace and strode through the hallway and stepped into the kitchen. I froze when Greyson's friend turned to me. His eyebrow flicked up, and his eyes trailed from my bare toes up to my face. A smile spread over his full lips as he gazed at me lasciviously.

This guy was pretty. Attractive in an in-your-face type way. Why didn't I want to ride his bones?

At least he was offering a kind smile. All I got from Greyson were moody looks.

"How are you, darling?" he said in a low, sexy tone that did absolutely nothing to me.

I blinked at him and took a seat. "Great, thanks," I said with forced cheer.

"I'm making dinner just for you." He winked.

"For little ol' me? You shouldn't have," I said the words in an exaggeratedly sweet tone. He was full of cow shit. I could smell it a mile away. That didn't stop me from seeing how far he was willing to take it. I pressed my arms closer together, glad that I'd left the top two buttons of the shirt undone. When I leaned forward a little, the draft that caressed my chest told me my cleavage was on display.

Daniel's smile spread, and he set the plates aside before sliding to my side of the island. I didn't move from my purposefully provocative position. The interest in his eyes was a balm to my hurt pride. Greyson was doing a number on me with his back and forth. Maybe he wasn't attracted to me . . .

I quickly pushed that thought aside as I recalled the multiple erections he'd pushed against me. No, he wanted me. He just didn't *want* to. It didn't take a genius to figure out his aversion to fae, but when he'd looked at me with such hate after kissing me so passionately, it'd hurt more than any pain Jaden had put me through in our entire relationship.

Daniel leaned a hip against the lip of the counter, and I craned my neck to stare into his pretty face. A foot separated us, but the distance lessened as he leaned close enough for me to see the black flecks in his eyes.

"It smells delicious. What are you making?" I licked my dry lips. I expected *some* type of reaction from my body, but there was absolutely nothing.

His long fingers lifted, and the pad of his thumb caressed my chin, nearing my lip with a slow brush.

"I made spaghetti." Before the thumb touched my lip, his hand was knocked away.

I whipped around to see Greyson glaring at Daniel, his eye twitching. A dent appeared between Daniel's eyebrows before they shuttered, and a wide grin took place of the downturn of his lips.

Greyson's arm brushed my side as he moved to sit in the

chair farthest away from me. My nipples pebbled at the slight, almost nonexistent touch. I tensed and didn't move from my position even though I wanted to straighten and cover myself at the heated look Greyson sent my peeking cleavage.

"What have you been up to?" I casually said to Greyson as Daniel stepped away and turned to the stove. I was still angry at the way he'd left me, but I was trying not to let it affect me. Anyway, I liked seeing him get all irate.

Greyson grunted in answer. I shrugged and turned back to the nicer . . . wolf? "You're a wolf, too, yes?"

Daniel turned away from the plates he was scooping spaghetti onto and flashed me a smile. "Yes. The best Unnatural species there is." He added a wink. He was ridiculous.

"If you say so," I said doubtfully. There were tons of Unnaturals. I was sure there were cooler ones than wolves . . . I peeked over at Greyson. Though, I may have been building a preference for them.

I forced my eyes away, but not quick enough before he met them. Irritation shadowed his face, and he pushed off the chair violently. The metal screeched against the floor, and I winced.

Greyson slammed open a cabinet. Bottles upon bottles of alcohol were set in a meticulous line. He grabbed the neck of one before grabbing a decanter.

I turned away before he caught me watching. Instead, I was left staring into Daniel's smirking face. I narrowed my eyes at the knowing look as he set my plate in front of me.

"Thanks," I said slowly and blinked innocently. I was trying to play off the gawking he'd caught me doing.

Greyson's chair scraped again as he sat, and Daniel put his plate down before turning to grab his own. Instead of sitting in the seat next to me, Daniel settled across from me.

"Let me know what you think," he said with a wink.

I rolled my eyes. If Eliza was here, she'd have her nose up at this guy or would be laughing her ass off. While I liked to play along, she liked to call the bullshit.

I twirled my fork into the spaghetti and scooped it into my mouth. "This is so good," I said, ignoring the pinch in my jaw.

Well, I tried to. It sounded more like a garble as I stuffed my face. I slurped another long noodle into my mouth. The tangy taste combined with the meat sauce was perfect. From the tickle on my face, I knew I was a mess, but there was no one I was trying to impress. I forced my eyes not to move to the gruff, hulking wolf eating a chair away from me and focused on the delicious food.

Not that men couldn't cook, but it was a rare sight to find. Being dropped in a place where two men cooked? It was a goddamned miracle.

CHAPTER 15
GREYSON

I WANTED TO BEAT DANIEL'S FACE UNTIL IT WAS bloody. I eyed Camilla and hid the snort of disgust at the smile in her eyes every time she looked at him. Currently, she was swallowing down the spaghetti like she'd never had anything so good. She hadn't reacted like that to the omelet I made her.

My fingers curled around the utensil, but I regulated my strength before it bent. I shoveled more food in my mouth as I watched her eat with her jaw working gingerly. Guilt mingled with the anger at the blush of bruises cresting on her face, but even beaten black and blue, she was gorgeous.

Daniel was another thing entirely. He'd already given me that smug look he gave when he had a woman where he wanted her. It hadn't helped the desire to bash his face.

"So, how is it, knowing you're fae spawn?" I observed them over the lip of my drink.

Camilla's grin widened, and she waved her fork at Daniel. "Quite the same as I'm sure it feels knowing y'all are wolf spawn."

Daniel leaned forward. I'd witnessed his woman-hunting

style before. He liked to overwhelm women with his proximity and teasing touches. They always fell for it. In all the years I'd seen him turn the charm toward someone, he never failed. It seemed the case was the same with Camilla. It made me fucking livid.

Turning away, I gripped the neck of the bottle, poured three fingers of whiskey, and threw it back like it was a shot. The burn did nothing to assuage the clenching in my chest. Nor the rage bubbling.

Daniel lifted his arm and touched her slightly damp hair. My lip curled to show some teeth. I hadn't done that in so long, the sensation felt foreign. It was a silent warning. No way in any fucking world would Daniel get his hands on Boots. I forbade it.

Daniel froze, evidently seeing me from the corner of his eyes. If he'd had his wolf, his instincts would have urged him to stay as still as possible, but I took the victory when he snatched his hand back and kept his eyes away from her perfect breasts.

Fuck, how I wanted to suckle them into my mouth and . . . I groaned and adjusted in my chair to relieve the tightening at the front of my jeans.

Camilla looked between Daniel and me, her eyebrows squeezed together. I scowled at her and turned back to my food, waiting until she turned away so I could watch her again.

"Are you trying to black out?" she asked. I ignored her humor-infused question and refilled my glass before throwing back another. "Can werewolves get drunk? Or do you need some nifty plant the way fae do?"

Daniel hummed and answered before I could. "Our other half is able to burn through the effects of alcohol quickly, but with the shift tied, we feel the effects a little longer. Wolfsbane affects Unnaturals with an animal form similar to fae. It lowers inhibition and creates a drunk-like feeling that lasts a very long time. Though there are some Unnaturals that react as if wolfsbane is poison—"

"Enough story time," I snapped, irritated at the chattiness between the pair. Wolfsbane would obliterate any reservations I had, to the extent that it would land me in her bed. Which was why I needed to stay far, far away from it for the foreseeable future.

"Well, this got awkward," she sang, her twang drawing out the words. I pressed my lips together at the twitch of my cock. She hopped off the chair and took her plate to the sink and turned on the faucet.

"Leave that to me, darling." Daniel reached out to touch her lower back, but at the screech of my chair, he retreated.

"He does dishes, too," she said, impressed. "Thanks for dinner. See you later, Daniel."

She shot me a look I couldn't read and traipsed out of the room with bare feet. It took everything in me not to trail after her.

"What the fuck was all that?" I snapped when I turned back to my beta.

Daniel's eyebrow twitched. "You're asking me? If I didn't know any better, I'd say you were jealous." He straightened, and his gaze flitted away from mine as he gentled his tone. "You can't let pussy confuse you. You know the consequences the last time that happened."

Rage at the idea that she was just pussy trilled through me. I filled my glass again and glared at him. "That's not even close to what's happening here," I said, seething.

"Then what the fuck?"

I combed through my brain to figure out what to say. "We can't let her get suspicious. If both of us are coming onto her, she'll wonder what's going on. I had it under control, she was slipping."

"I figured if you weren't going to seduce answers out of her, I would." He shrugged and turned to pile more food onto his plate. "I'm glad you got it handled. Sorry I doubted you, Alpha. I can tell she's attracted to you. It shouldn't be hard to get her between the sheets."

I inclined my head and grunted, forcing myself not to correct him. I had her where I wanted, but then I pulled away when my conscience made a showing.

I glowered down at my swirling drink and chugged it again. The shots were beginning to go to my head. I pressed the palm of my hand to my left eye as it unfocused.

"Oh, and I made sure Tara stays away. She thinks she's giving you time to cool off." Daniel snorted and shook his head. "That she-wolf is one twisted pup."

"I know," I muttered, looking out of the window above the sink. The light was fading from the sky. "I need to clear that up. She's not my mate regardless of how much she tries to act like it."

"You've never mentioned mates before." Daniel smirked. "Once we get our wolf, maybe you'll finally find yours."

"You first," I retorted. I was neither for nor against being mated, but I wouldn't be searching for it either.

"Ha! As if I would get tied down." He chuckled and cleared away our plates before beginning the dishes. I shook my head as he continued to chuckle.

I gripped my glass in one hand and the half-empty bottle of Jack in the other. The glass clanged as I thumped it down and drank directly from the bottle. Pushing off the chair, I moved to the couch in the living room. The cushion molded to my body, and I tilted my head back after taking another chug.

Daniel was right. The chase of screwing someone was what killed my family. I'd wanted to fuck that fae for fun. It was simply a bet, but I hadn't realized she'd had a male companion who hadn't taken her mingling with werewolves lightly.

Little had I known he would take it out on my pack.

My stomach churned as I thought back to that dark time. My life had been torn asunder, and I'd become alpha that night.

CHAPTER 16
CAMILLA

I JERKED OUT OF MY HALF-SLEEP AT THE SOUND OF A crash. Grabbing my phone, I checked the time. It was past midnight. Who was up this late?

I stumbled to my feet, and shuffling to the door, I slid it open and peeked out. There were no other sounds, but curiosity urged me to investigate. I crept to the stairs, and curses filtered to my ears.

I made it to the base of the stairs and down the hall. Turning the corner, I found Greyson sitting on the couch. His shoulders were slumped, and his head rested in his hands with his fingers buried in his hair. He was the vision of torment.

I clenched my hands into tight fists, fighting the desire to get near him. To comfort him. When that didn't work, I gripped my bruised arm and poked at it, but I still found myself inching close. I angled to his side and touched his shoulder.

Every muscle in his body tensed, and I waited for him to shove me away but to my surprise, he didn't. I gave into the weird need to comfort him and sat beside him, squeezing his shoulder. I sat there as he rubbed his face.

My eyes widened at the glass shattered on the floor. He'd chucked the bottle of alcohol against the wall. What was wrong with him? He'd been acting off the entire dinner. Almost belligerent. I'd wanted to straight-out ask him, but I hadn't been in a mood for grunts as responses.

"Are you okay?"

"No," he said crisply. I tensed and moved away to go back to my room. I wasn't going to stay for his attitude. Greyson's hand flashed out and squeezed my thigh. I froze. "I'm thinking about my family."

The way he slurred his speech a little told me he was feeling the booze. I would too if I'd practically chugged an entire bottle of hard liquor. He sat up and fixed me with unfocused glassy eyes.

"What about them?" I cautiously asked. I kept waiting for him to push me away, but he didn't, and that surprised me even more.

"Their deaths," he slurred, and I tensed. "It was my fault." The way his voice cracked created a fissure in my chest.

"I'm sure that's not the case," I said softly.

"It is," he snapped. I jumped at the lash. "Sorry," he said, rubbing his face. Why did he think it was his fault?

Greyson was eaten up with guilt, and now I understood where it stemmed from. It became more obvious with each second I spent around him, but at the same time, I couldn't imagine him hurting anyone. He'd treated Ann and her kids with such care. The last people I imagined him hurting was his family.

"Did you kill them?" I asked and clenched my hands to keep from touching him. He had no qualms about feeling *me* up though. His hand squeezed my thigh, his nails rasping the seam of my jeans. I cleared my throat and barely refrained from turning toward him.

Greyson didn't answer my question. Instead, he pierced me with his dilated eyes. I wiggled on the couch as he stared me down as if deciding if he wanted to speak.

"If they loved you, they wouldn't want you to be torturing yourself this way," I continued.

"I was close to them," he finally said, releasing me from his thrall when he looked away. He caressed my thigh slowly. Heat built, and I squirmed into the couch. My eyes were drawn to the growing bulge in his jeans.

"What about your pack? They seem very protective of you, especially Ann." My shoulders tightened at my sharp words. I wished I could take them back. I pressed my lips together as he continued running his thumb over the upper side of my leg, coaxing a throb from my pussy.

"I've known her since she was born." He surprised me by answering my unasked question. "I watched her grow up. She's family."

I nodded, even though I wanted to let him know that she didn't see him as innocently as he seemed to think. There was a part of Ann that saw him as the gruff, caring man he was toward her.

My chest twisted. That gentleness had never been directed at me. Even when he wasn't being snappy toward me, I couldn't help but feel his disapproval every time he pierced me with those lush eyes.

"How old are you?"

"Three hundred and sixteen," he answered easily. I gaped at his answer, doing the math in my head. Magic was around until about two hundred and ninety years ago. He'd been a couple years shy of missing maturity. "Two years after I reached maturity, they were killed."

I didn't have to ask who *they* were. "Was it your mom and dad, or did you have siblings?"

"I had—" Greyson's throat visibly worked as he swallowed. "I had a younger brother. He tried to help and was also killed."

I ached to ask for more details, but I didn't. Mostly because I noticed how he rubbed his eyes as if the alcohol was beginning to leave his system. Even his gaze seemed clearer.

Greyson flashed me a look and then scowled at the wall. Oh, he was definitely beginning to get back to himself. Sharing time was over. I should get back to my room before he acted like his lovely self.

Setting my hand on his, I squeezed. The large, rough hand was warm, and flutters filled my stomach. It took me a second to articulate a sentence.

"I'm sorry you've lost so much," I said, brushing my fingers over the back where the veins flexed. I cleared my throat as I continued with the light touch, wanting his skin imprinted on mine.

Greyson's hand suddenly clenched mine, and he jerked me to him. I slammed against his hard chest. The heat of his skin radiated into me and made goosebumps rise all over my body. My breasts rubbed against his hard chest and caused sweet friction. An unintentional sound slipped from my mouth.

"I need you," he said with a growl, and his lips slammed down onto mine. With deft movements, he took my lips, lapping at my tongue. We broke apart second later with a gasp.

He gripped my thighs and dragged me closer. In the same movement, he dropped to his knees. Air left my lungs as he unbuttoned my jeans and tugged them down in swift, jerky motions. I tipped my hips to help him get them off. Once he'd gotten them off, he pulled me to the edge of the couch.

"Bare—just as I like." A wicked grin curled his lips. Then his mouth was where I'd wanted it since I met him. His warm tongue delved between slit.

"You can't get away with being back and forth." I gasped and fell back into the couch. *My goodness*, he was magnificent at this. "I thought you didn't want—ah." I made a strange noise as he flicked his tongue. It flattened and traveled to my bud. He nipped the nerves, and I yelped in a mix of pleasure and pain. A throaty moan escaped my lips, and I gripped his hair, forcing him closer to my pussy.

Greyson engulfed my hips with his large hands, and his fingers dug into my ass as he tilted me toward his mouth. The tunneling and flicks of his tongue combined with the pressure of his lips pushing against my core was heaven.

Whimpering, I gripped his hair harder, curling my fingers into the dark strands. The build of my orgasm crested suddenly with a skillful nip at my clit. I might have yelled out his name, but I wasn't sure because I blacked out for a split second.

Without warning, a door slammed, and he'd pulled up my jeans so fast, I barely processed it as he moved. It gave me whiplash, and the afterglow of the best orgasm I'd ever had faded as I lay on the couch in a confused puddle.

I blinked at Greyson, who leaned against the wall farthest from me, his chest rising and falling with rapid huffs. Springing to my feet, I prepared to deliver a snappy retort before exiting, but when I turned, I froze.

Tara stared back at me with the same shock I felt. She sneered, and I smiled, knowing my jeans were unbuttoned.

"Why the fuck are you wearing my clothes?"

My stomach fell. I hadn't known she was the packmate he'd taken the clothes from. I thought it'd been Ann, but not her. She cut me off before I could say anything and glared at Greyson. I had the strangest need to get in her line of sight.

Tara snarled before lunging at me.

CHAPTER 17
GREYSON

IN TWO QUICK STRIDES, I GRIPPED CAMILLA AND shoved her behind me. I caught Tara's raised fist and glared down at her. Fucking Tara. Right when I decided to give in and fuck Boots, she strode into my house like she owned it. If my wolf had been able to come out, I would have torn her to pieces.

She tried to tug out of my grip, but I held on to her, knowing she hadn't snapped out of her rage by the look in her blue eyes.

"Enough," I yelled with a growl. Tara took a step back and snapped her lips shut. Good. I offered another warning look, and she finally dipped her head deferentially. I hadn't pulled rank in so long, it felt strange. "What do you want?"

Tara flinched, but I didn't feel bad. She was on my last nerve. I could still taste Camilla's sweet pussy on my lips, and I wanted to be done with this so I could go back for another taste.

"Mrs. Jacobson is in labor."

"Fuck," I muttered and jumped to action. Pulling out my

phone, I called the doctor. The phone rang once before going to voicemail. I tried again and had the same results. "No answer."

"We can take her to the hospital?" Tara offered.

"And chance her having the child in the car?" I ran my hands through my hair. What was I going to do? I paced and itched to grab another whiskey bottle to drown in, but I couldn't fail a packmate.

"I've delivered calves on my parents' farm," Camilla said shakily. I glanced at her as she slid her hands into her pocket, nervousness in her eyes. "It can't be too different, right?"

Relief and gratitude filled me at her offer. I fought the urge to push her back onto the couch and lick her all over.

"That's the best we have," I said and wished I could have chosen different words. Camilla turned away but not before I noticed the hurt flash in her eyes. "Let's go," I said instead and didn't wait for her to follow. I was too ashamed.

I slipped into my truck and watched Camilla stumble out of the house in my boots again. She was adorable as she waddled as quickly as she could to the vehicle.

The passenger door opened and slammed shut. I clenched my hands around the wheel so I wouldn't forcibly remove Tara. I wanted Camilla next to me.

As soon as the back door shut, I took off toward the Jacobsons' house, racing down the familiar road. It was bumpier than the one to Ann's, as it was deeper into the land.

Camilla cursed from the back seat, and I tried not to grin. Tara eyed me, and I wiped the look off my face and scowled.

"Can you shut up, fucking hillbilly," she snapped.

The wheel creaked under my hands. But before I could do anything I may or may not regret, Camilla startled me by filling the car with her laughter.

"Girl, you got issues." Camilla chortled.

I smirked, and my hand flashed out to shove Tara back in her seat. I could tell she was about to throw herself over the seat. Tara huffed and sat back. I'd have to keep an eye on her. She was unpredictable, and as soon as my back was turned, she'd go after Boots.

I wasn't looking forward to addressing this little role she liked playing. I needed to make it clear she needed to stop acting like my mate.

We arrived at the Jacobsons' in record time. The door was already open. Jake Jacobson leaned against the porch, worry seeping from him. When Camilla stepped out of the car, he shoved off, about to charge her.

"No," I ordered sharply. Jake was a year younger than me, but I was still alpha. I gave him a warning look, and he backed off.

Mrs. Jacobson was Jake's great-great-great-niece. He lived in his own house a mile out from this one because he liked to keep an eye on his descendants.

I waved Camilla forward, watching Jake as I did. I didn't want to start something with him, but he'd always been unpredictable. We followed Tara to a dimly lit bedroom where Mrs. Jacobson thrashed and moaned.

I peered at a nervous Camilla. Alcohol had once again failed me. If I hadn't had any, I wouldn't have spilled my guts. I couldn't fathom I'd told her about my family, but now that I had, I wanted to know her thoughts... on everything. When Mrs. Jacobson cried out again, Camilla burst into motion. She shoved up the nightgown as she spoke.

"Howdy, Mrs. Jacobson. I'm Camilla. You're doing great, we can get through this together." I was in awe at her control even though I could sense how unsure she was. "Breathe," she added when Mrs. Jacobson went into another contraction.

Camilla pushed her legs wider, slipping on the long gloves Tara handed her. Camilla mumbled her thanks with an edge of sarcasm. Tara narrowed her eyes.

My eyes trailed back to Camilla. Her swift professional movements made my dick harden. I cleared my throat. Not the time.

"Where's her husband and other kids?" I asked Tara.

"On their way. He'd taken the kids out to get ice cream."

"Greyson, hold her hand and try to get her to stay still," Camilla called. I immediately moved to Trix Jacobson's side and gripped her shoulder in one hand. Sweat poured off her. "Tara, get me all the towels you can find and disinfected scissors."

Surprisingly, Tara did as Camilla ordered without me having to push her to it.

I focused on Camilla as she concentrated. She was phenomenal. She moved in quick, efficient motions. Grabbing one of the towels, she spread it under Mrs. Jacobson, then tugged the sheet over her legs to offer privacy. The hand gripping mine squeezed harder, and I looked down at her strained expression. I tried to smile, but her eyes were so glazed and filled with tears, I knew she didn't register my attempt.

Mrs. Jacobson cried out and her neck strained with her shout. Frantic eyes skid across the room. The little fae muttered under her breath, eyes narrowed on the woman's . . . areas.

I grimaced.

"Push," Camilla ordered.

The next hour went by in a blur. I forced my mind to blank as nails dug into my arm. Poor woman was a panting mess. I didn't bother trying to say anything to the birthing mother, she'd already snapped at me. Camilla's narrow-eyed look had made me snap my mouth shut.

She worked efficiently, coaxing Mrs. Jacobson with encouraging words and letting her know when she needed to exert herself.

This was out of my fucking element. Air puffed out of my lungs and I longed to tug at the collar of my shirt. Camilla exhaled sharply. I met her eyes and my racing heart settled. She leaned forward, shoving Mrs. Jacobson's legs open with her shoulders as she hunched.

My teeth clicked together, and I forced away my eyes. The strange need to shove myself between them and throw Camilla over my shoulder rode me.

It was illogical and stupid.

The pained whimper was what snapped me back to the woman. I removed my hand from her shoulder as she clutched the bedsheets. Camilla's brow creased, and she looked up and smiled at Mrs. Jacobson.

Camilla gaped at my hovering hand stretched toward her.

I brushed away the bead of sweat on her forehead before curling my fingers and forcing myself to the corner of the room.

Tara's judgmental mutter made my teeth snap and I bared them at her.

"You're so close." Camilla's voice was soothing. A balm to my soul. I knew she wasn't speaking to me, but I selfishly took those words within myself and closed my eyes acting like they were directed at me. "You're almost there. One more time."

There was a screech and then a cry broke out. Camilla grinned wide and success shone on her expression as she maneuvered before lifting a wiggling bloody baby.

Tears dripped down Mrs. Jacobson's face. She met Camilla's eyes. "Thank you," she rasped in an overused voice.

Tara grabbed the cub and wrapped it up in a towel before setting it into Mrs. Jacobson's arms. My stomach lurched at the bloody bundle, and I swallowed hard. Camilla stepped away with her arms wrapped in a fresh towel. She looked in my direction. Ah, she wanted to wash off. I nodded to the side door where the bathroom was. The faucet sounded as she cleaned off.

"Stay here and help," I told Tara. She scowled, but I ignored her and strode to the bathroom entrance as Camilla stepped out with freshly washed hands. Her eyes rounded when she found me looming at the door frame.

Her throat bobbed and we stared at each other. Tense seconds stretched to feel like minutes until I lifted my hand, reaching for her face.

Her eyebrows furrowed and I redirected my hand behind my neck, as if that was my goal the entire time.

What was wrong with me?

I frowned and jerked my head toward the door. She swept past me, head held high and eyes reflecting the confusion I felt.

It was easy to keep up with her stride. When the front door came in my line of sight, I gave into my desire to touch her.

Pressing my palm to the small of her back, I directed her to the car. She was unusually silent as we climbed into the truck. The crying of the newborn filtered out of the window.

We arrived at the house without a word said between us. Gratitude bubbled in my chest. I wanted to express how grateful I was, but the words wouldn't come out, so I kept them in. I waved her into the house as I held the door open. She paused at the threshold, indecision playing on her face. Her teeth clicked.

"Who is Tara to you?" She hesitated before continuing. "I can tell there's an unreciprocated obsession. Are you sure y'all aren't together?"

"She's nothing more than a part of my pack." I left out that she was my go-to fuck buddy. She gave me a look as if she understood there was something I wasn't saying. I stepped forward, and she stumbled back. The pulse fluttered at her neck. As brave as she acted, she couldn't hide her nerves. I was so close she had to crane her neck to look up at me. "You were amazing."

I caught her mouth with my lips. Crowding her until her back hit the wall. I nudged her legs open and pulled her off her feet to nestle between her legs. A sexy groan rasped up her throat. My cock hardened painfully. Tilting my hips, I thrust. She moaned into my mouth; the sound inflamed me further. If there was no clothing between us, I'd be deep inside her.

Camilla buried one hand in my hair while the other gripped my shoulder. The sexual tension between us was palpable. By her reaction, it wasn't just me it was driving crazy. She needed me as much as I needed her. Fuck it, I was done denying my desires.

My balls were heavy from need, and I ground my dick against her ruthlessly. Her wetness made the juncture of her jeans damp. I was going to fuck her right here against the wall.

Then my cell phone rang. I tensed and cursed. Camilla softened her grip on me until it slid away. I frowned at the absence.

"I have to take this," I said, setting her feet down. I pressed my lips to hers, hard. "We aren't done." I pulled away, her wide eyes angled up at me, and she nodded tightly. Unable to let her go, I pressed a second quick kiss to her lips. Camilla turned and stumbled out of the foyer after slipping the borrowed shoes off, then made her way upstairs.

I answered without looking at the caller ID. I grunted into the phone.

"Greyson, I was checking in on you."

I tensed to the point of shattering when reality rushed back. "Are you doubting me?" I said in a sharp tone.

"No," Tristin replied slowly, and I could feel his confused shock.

"I have to go," I muttered before tossing my phone on the stand in the entrance hallway. Shoving my fingers through my hair, I tilted my head back. My heart raced from the remnant feeling of the kiss. Tension bunched my shoulders. Nerves tingled through my veins. The walls were closing in on me. I squeezed my eyes shut. I needed to get my head back on straight. What was I thinking?

As much as I craved Camilla, she was a means to an end. It was too late to go back, or even make my mistakes up to her. She would hate me for the lies and deception.

Without warning, my ears popped, and I jerked in surprise. As my legs trembled, I splayed my hand on the wall to hold myself up. Pain shivered through me, and my muscles burned. What the hell was going on . . .?

My body twisted and reformed. It was like stretching for the first time when I hadn't been able to for eons.

It hurt so fucking good.

I strained my legs and worked to keep control as the almost forgotten feeling of the shift overtook me.

CHAPTER 18
CAMILLA

A SHIVER GHOSTED THROUGH THE AIR, AND I RUBBED my arms at the sudden draft. The tingle rose every hair on my body, and I rolled my shoulders to force away the odd sensation.

An elongated eerie howl sounded from outside. Sliding off the bed, I strode to the window and pushed it open as more bays exploded through the night. A bad feeling prickled the back of my neck. I needed to find Greyson. I hugged myself and took one step before all hell broke loose.

The door ricocheted off the wall, and the wood splintered. Greyson stood at the threshold. My eyes widened as I took in his naked form. A scrap of denim was around his ankle, but my eyes roved right back up to his hard cock. My body flushed with heat.

"Why are you naked?" I breathed, although I wasn't complaining. Another howl sounded. "Did you hear those wolves?" I snapped my fingers. "Can you talk to them since you're a werewolf?"

In a swift motion, quicker than I'd ever seen him move, Greyson stalked to me. His large hand gripped my hip, and he pressed his heavy cock into my stomach. I tensed, confused, but utterly turned on by his dick. His eyes glinted in the lighting. The gold had almost overpowered the green shade of his eyes. An eye color uniquely his.

Before I could speak, he caught my mouth, devouring my lips.

No, he claimed them. He'd never kissed me with such desperation. I'd never known what being plundered was like, but that was exactly what he did.

He claimed my mouth and made it his with every flick and nip. My pussy became soaked. His fingers curled into my back, and I felt sharpness . . . like claws. They grazed down my back, and shivers erupted at the surprisingly gentle touch.

A needy moan sounded, and I realized it came from me. All sense was blurring. Greyson's fingers dug into the back of my legs, and then he lifted me like I was a feather. He held me suspended with just his hands, holding me tightly to his body.

I arched against his hard length as a snarl ripped from his lips. There was a tug and he tore the jeans in one smooth jerk, then I was bare from the waist down. I grunted at the flush of heat to my core. My eyes widened at how effortless it was. That was so goddamn hot.

His head fell back when our flesh touched. His dick nudged and pressed against my pubic bone, and then it became difficult for me to form coherent thoughts. Greyson squeezed his eyes tightly and went taut.

"Do you want this?" he rasped, his chest heaving from his labored breaths. I wiggled my hips, needing him to thrust inside me.

There was no doubt about it. I'd wanted him from day one, and the teasing simply intensified that need.

"Yes." I gripped his hair and pulled him down to my lips. A pleased sound rumbled from his chest. I had to arch forward since his hold on my hips didn't allow me any movement.

Greyson flexed his grip on my thighs, the entirety of his hands engulfing them. He strode to the bed with me clutching his biceps. I tried moving against him. I needed more of him. My wet pussy coated him, and the slide of his head against my clit made shivers erupt.

He growled again and set me down into the plush edge of the bed. Panting, I stared up at his glinting, savage eyes.

"Fuck me, Grey," I whimpered, and his huge cock slammed into me. I yelled at the full sensation, my channel offering no resistance as he slid in. I'd never been so full. So overtaken.

He slid out slowly and rammed back into me. My neck strained as I craned my head back, mouth open on a silent cry. He did it again, and his fingers tightened—stinging. Pleasure and pain mixed, but at the intensifying pinch, I tensed slightly even though I wanted him to keep pounding into me.

I patted his hands. "Gentle."

He froze over me, a low rumbling filling the space. "Fuck. I hurt you."

As I gazed into his lust-filled eyes, I noticed an eeriness to them. His pupils were expanded similarly to an animals. He had access to his shift, but how . . .?

Thoughts left me as he flipped me in a smooth motion and set me on top of him without disconnecting us. Instead of gripping my hips, he dug his fingers into the bedsheets at his sides. The material ripped as soon as I slipped down his cock and seated myself with a moan. The fullness was life-altering. I cried out at the sensation and wiggled on his him. His neck strained, and a growl ripped through the room.

Greyson's hip jerked up, and I took the cue to undulate up and down. He reached up and gripped the edge of my borrowed shirt before tearing it open. Buttons flew all over the place. I was glad to be rid of *her* clothing.

His fingers slipped to my breasts, urging me to move faster. I quickened my pace, but that didn't seem to be fast enough for Greyson because he thrust up until I bounced in a steady rhythm. My head fell back at the incoming climax.

Whimpers, his name, and nonsensical mutters fell from my lips as the wave compounded. A trembled coasted up my legs and I tensed, meeting his eyes. There was a softness reflecting there as he beheld me, and it sent me over the cliff. My pussy tugged hard at his jerking cock as every twitch of him inside me wrenched a moan from my soul. Greyson groaned, eyelids shuttering closed.

My throat tightened at the emotion building in my chest. The softening in my heart was frightening, but I didn't want to fight it. Not right now.

I fell onto his rapidly rising chest.

Eliza would be proud, I really *had* ridden him like a cowgirl. A smile flitted across my lips. I languished on top of him as I caught my breath. He seemed to be doing the same under me, his heaving chest incrementally relaxing.

"Dammit, we didn't use protection." I huffed with a laugh and snuggled deeper into his arms. "The last thing we need is you getting me pregnant."

A change came over him. Greyson tensed everywhere, even though his dick remained hard inside me. He shoved me off, and the force rolled me to the side. I grunted and was glad I had the bed to catch me.

He jumped to his feet and paced from one end of the room

to the other. He flashed a look at me, and the hateful edge to it tore my heart in half.

"Why are you acting like an ass again?"

"I can't ejaculate with anyone but my future mate. And that's not you," he spat.

I jerked into a seating position so fast, the room spun. His emotional shifts gave me whiplash. I fought the building pressure behind my eyes.

"You don't need to be a fucking jerk. I was in here minding my own business when you came in, junk swinging, and had your way with me. I was gladly an active participant, but don't put it on me."

"You're a fucking menace," he hissed. Then I watched that fine ass flex as he walked out.

I'd thought Jaden had issues. This guy had nothing on him. I tossed myself on my back. Why did I have a thing for bad boys? Every heartbeat shuddered with pain. *Why?*

Exhaling sharply, I took stock of my well fucked body. My hand trailed down to my pussy. The wetness was still there. I moaned at my grazing touch. Frustration made me ball my fists and slam them at my sides.

After wallowing for a bit, I figured I should get dressed before he came in huffing and puffing again.

I pushed off the bed and found my borrowed, ripped clothing piled on the floor. A small—no, a large part of me was absurdly pleased. Not only because it was hot, but because it had been Tara's.

How had he gotten her clothes anyway? I tensed, and the doubt that they were something attached itself to my brain. The possessive way she treated him, the fact that he had access to her clothes . . . All the signs were there, despite what he'd said. He could be lying . . .

That goddamned mutt. He better have not lied.

My teeth clicked together.

There was only one way to be sure.

Naked as the day I was born, I strutted out of the room. Snooping was bad. That was a given, but if I was being made a fool of, I needed to know

I'd never finished exploring the rest of the house like I'd wanted to. I strode deeper into the hall. There were four rooms other than mine on both sides of the hall. I opened each door and peeked in. They were completely bare. I went to the door on the other side of mine and pushed it open.

I flicked the light as I stepped in and almost fell on my face. Catching myself, I gaped at the disarray of the bedroom. There were clothes thrown all over the place. My nose wrinkled. Had Tara's bedroom been next to mine this entire time? If that was the case, why had she been gone the last few days?

Stop getting ahead of yourself. First, find out if the room is even hers.

The chill of the encroaching night seemed to slip through the windowsill, and I shivered, crossing my arms over my bare breasts as I inched to the drawers.

The clothing piled on top of the dresser was a similar style to the ones I'd borrowed. My stomach soured. Closing my eyes, I pushed past the pressure building behind.

It was undoubtedly hers.

The chill in the room made me shiver and I glanced at the open drawer.

The last thing I wanted was to wear her clothing, but

honestly, I wanted my skin covered. Vulnerability spilled through my veins.

Had Greyson used me?

He always seemed so disgusted after giving into our crazy chemistry. It wasn't like I wanted to be his mate or anything like that, but did he have to be such a goddamned jerk? The words he said stung as they swirled in the back of my head. He didn't need to lie to me about whatever messed up relationship he had with Tara.

Embarrassment heated my face.

I was the one encroaching on her space, no wonder she loathed me.

An elongated howl came from outside, and I shivered. I'd never seen a shifted werewolf, and I wasn't planning to anytime soon.

Yanking the handle, it took a couple of tries before the drawer opened. The reason it was stuck was explained when I saw how full it was. I shook my head in disgust. I woulda been whooped if I'd let my room get this messy. I never thought Momma coming after me to clean my room so much when I was younger would be something I would ever be grateful for. Yet, here I was, thanking those very grueling fights between me and her.

My lips quirked at the memory of a specific one we'd had when I'd thrown it in her face that she never went after Cosmo. I'd claimed it was because he was their *actual* son. I was being a turd, but it was the way I used to deal.

I'd long since realized that many sons got treated like porcelain glass by their mothers. Sons could do no wrong. Not only that, but knowing your parents loved you, no matter where you came from or how different you looked, made all the difference.

I pulled on a pair of shorts and grabbed *another* button down. I didn't need anything fancy. I just needed to be covered as I made my escape. My head was pushing through the collar when a floorboard creaked.

"Why are you in my room?"

And that confirmed it.

I braced myself before looking at her. Her head tilted slightly to the side, and her eyes seemed almost fully black with her expanded pupils. She was also completely naked.

Tara inched forward and froze. "You smell like him."

A snarl ripped from her chest, and she stalked toward me. I stepped back until I was against the window. I wasn't above sticking my head out and yelling for help. I didn't know how this wolf stuff worked. Would Greyson even understand me if he was in his werewolf form? I didn't think they were two separate entities...

Fur sprouted down her arms, her body expanding. My eyes widened, but I couldn't look away as her nails darkened and became claws. She seemed to be in some partial wolf state. She bared her teeth, flashing long fangs. I swallowed hard as my heart went into overdrive.

"I'll enjoy ripping you apart for touching what's mine."

I didn't even know he was yours.

I couldn't get the words out of my throat, though. I also wanted to tell her that it wasn't very woman power-esque to blame the chick who knew nothing. She should be giving Greyson hell.

Her body fell into itself and fur burst out of every inch of her skin, covering her entire body. Then a wolf way larger than your normal wild wolf stood in her place. The smooth brown coat left me in awe.

Her ears flicked back, and her legs bunched before she flew at me. I ducked just in time, and she crashed through the window. I covered my head as glass shattered.

I couldn't believe my luck. The dumbass had tossed herself through the barrier.

There was a canine cry, and I jumped to my feet to look out the window. The brown wolf shook herself off. If I hadn't moved in time, my body would be crumpled down there.

In the next moment, a gray wolf, bulkier than hers, came flying out of the trees. He didn't slow down and, instead, bowled her over. He then gripped her by the neck and dragged her into the forest.

I was left staring with my mouth open. That was Greyson. I knew it in my bones.

A singular glass piece jingled as it fell, and I jerked out of my shock. I'd thought fae were intense . . .

I was out of here. This back and forth had gone on long enough. After grabbing my phone and boots from the bedroom, I pounded down the steps, then stopped near the door when I remembered Cory. He may still need my blood to help him heal.

I stamped my foot before turning to the kitchen and jerking all the drawers open until I found a piece of paper and a pen. I scribbled my name and number down. There, that would be good enough.

The keys to the truck glinted on the island. I snatched them up and clutched them. The keys dug into my hand as I ran to the door, boots crunching the gravel underneath my heels. I eyed the surroundings, but there were no wolves to be seen. I slammed into the truck and jammed the key in, twisting it. The engine revved on, and I pushed into drive. Nerves made my movements frantic. This was my only chance at escape. They were too distracted with whatever wolfy thing they had going on. Pressing on the gas, the tires slid and jolted forward.

I took the road headed east and drove for ten minutes. The further I got, the more I relaxed.

The silence heightened my anxiety, so I clicked on the radio and tapped along to the beat. The distraction worked—for a moment.

When I was three miles or so away from the house, I peeked at the rearview mirror and saw the eerie reflection of animal eyes behind me. The glint slowly gained on me even though it was a good distance away. Shit. I stepped on the gas harder.

Greyson wouldn't catch me. His hot and cold routine had grown tedious, and I missed Eliza. Plus, I couldn't believe he'd lied to me.

He and Tara obviously had *something* despite his assurances. My heart twisted, but I quickly quieted it. Lies were shit. I wasn't about to be dragged into a bout of depression by another man. Believing Jaden's lies was all the stupidity I wanted on my conscience. When I'd found out he had been juggling multiple girlfriends, my pride and self-esteem had taken a blow. I'd finally gotten myself out of that mindset, and I wasn't getting back into it. No way.

I exhaled sharply as I bumped onto the main road. Thank Lord, I remembered which road led to civilization.

My mind worked overtime, and I puffed out my cheeks.

Before realizing I was gone, it was possible he was out there fucking Tara in wolf form. Nausea roiled my stomach, and I swallowed hard. *That* was probably who his mate was. Jealousy reared its head, and I grimaced. *Distraction.* I pulled my phone out and dialed Eliza.

"Hello," she rasped. Immediately, I knew something was wrong.

"Are you okay?"

"Cam? I turned fae."

My heart twisted for my friend, and I stomped on the gas, pushing the truck to a dangerous level. I'd been planning to ditch this car, but Eliza needed me—now. "I'm coming. Where are you?"

"At the house."

CHAPTER 19
GREYSON

She was leaving me?

My nose twitched at the receding scent from an exhaust pipe, and I slowed. My ear twitched in the direction of an engine. A very familiar engine. I snarled.

Running at breakneck speed, I pushed my hind legs hard, tapping into Unnatural speed. The engine roared as I kicked up gravel. It took a while to process what I was seeing. My truck's headlights were miles away down the road. My ears pointed forward as I focused everything I had on catching up to it. Camilla. I whined and pushed harder.

Gravel spit into the air as she accelerated.

Rage fused me, and I snarled.

Camilla, running away from me.

No.

I eyed the distance between the fading lights. My leg slipped on a rock and my steps stuttered. Fuck, I was too out of practice with this body. Eyeing the distance, I sped up, but now there was no way. She twisted onto the main paved road. I couldn't chance going into civilization as a wolf.

Dirt kicked up with my abrupt stop. I snarled and turned back to my house. If I hadn't had to drag fucking Tara away, I would have been on time.

I needed to track her down, but I couldn't get to her in my wolf form. I tore through branches that snagged my fur, unfazed by the sharp tugs. The forest's nightlife quieted as I rampaged through the foliage.

I trotted back to the house and shifted back. My bones cracked and expanded. I stretched out my arms. Happiness was the only emotion I should be feeling now. This was what I'd wanted. The ability to shift, but the heavy ball in my stomach didn't allow me enjoyment. That damn fae! I lopped through every room, confirming her absence.

There had been a small part of me that held onto hope, but she was gone. And she'd taken my truck.

I paced in irritation and anxiety when I caught her delicious scent mingling outside of Tara's room. What had she been doing in there? Fuck. I knew allowing Tara her own space would bite my ass one day. I buried my hands through my hair. Why was it biting my ass? I shouldn't care. Magic was back, there was no longer need to be around Camilla. The hint of her scent teased me again. Tara had crashed through this window and I had no doubt she'd attacked Camilla. I clenched my hand so I wouldn't slam it into the wall. Now Camilla was gone.

A growl slipped free and I ground my molars.

The only reason I was going to go after her was because I still needed to give her to Tristan. Nothing else.

I stormed downstairs to grab a change of clothes. I donned them swiftly and made my way to the kitchen, the ravenous hunger refusing to be ignored. Food first and then I'd hunt her down. My plan formed and was decided as I combed through the fridge. Setting the lunch meat on the surface of the island, I saw something flutter at my peripheral. I snatched the scrap of paper and found her number scrawled across it. I snorted in disgust and dropped it.

Soft steps padded up behind me. "The bitch ran off then."

Lifting my nose, I tensed. Tara had the barest scent of Camilla. My eyelid twitched, and I whirled.

"You attacked Camilla." Her eyes widened, fear and blood scenting the air, telling me everything I needed to know. My eyes dropped to her bloody arm. I narrowed my eyes.

"Why did you attack *me*," Tara exploded, holding her arm.

A growl rumbled out of my chest. She froze and automatically bowed her head. I inhaled for more hints of Camilla's scent. Growling, I narrowed my eyes at Tara. She was fucking pissing me off. An itch climbed through my body. To go outside and begin my hunt for the woman with the smell I wanted to roll around on.

"What did you say to her?" I slowed my words menacingly.

"N-nothing." She took a step away from my stalk forward.

A wolf with a reddish pelt trotted into the house with his tail wagging. It distracted me enough to pull me out of my anger.

"Daniel," I said. His ears perked up as he panted and let out a short bark. I shook my head at him. "You'll never turn back."

His muzzle fell open in a wolf's grin. I'd thought he'd been joking when he'd told me he was staying in wolf form for weeks if we ever got our wolves back.

My cell rang, and I answered without looking. "What?"

"Greyson."

"Tristin," I said on a growl.

"This is a turn of events, but I'm still coming for that fae." I checked my strength before I crushed the phone. "Before, it was pure speculation, but I've gained the witches' trust, and it's true that there are experimentations underway to open a doorway to Faerie."

"Why do we need to? Magic is back," I said calmly—reasonably. When all I wanted was to rage.

"Those fucking fae need to pay. They hide away in their own world acting like we aren't from there, too. It's time they're put down the food chain where they belong," he spat.

Agitation made me growl. It was true. I knew the stories. The fae had forced most every Unnatural out to the human world centuries ago. Too long ago. They'd always thought they were superior. I remembered the smug look of that fae who had killed my family. He was probably hiding there . . .

I could choke the bastard. The image of his smug face was painted in my mind. Then my family's flashed to the forefront. Bitter anger squeezed my throat.

"I'll see you then," I snapped and clicked off. I would not think about the fact that I'd cringed from what I'd agreed to. I owed nothing to Camilla.

And there was no better time to hunt her down than now. I searched for Daniel's keys. His sports car was too flashy for me, but I was left without any other option since my truck had been stolen. My lips curled as I switched on my phone and swiped to the app that allowed you to find your "friends." Anticipating a move like this, when I'd had her cell, I'd accepted my own request to find her. I tapped on her name. It showed the blue dot moving toward the thick of the city.

The click of nails sounded on my hardwood floors, and another wolf crept into the house. My eyebrows lowered as a familiar scent filled my nose. I inhaled sharply. "Ann?"

I'd forgotten about the wolves who would mature as soon as they changed. The small gray wolf whined. She'd never shifted in her life. She must have been terrified when she started changing.

The kids.

Damn, Lawrence had been on the road and on his way back. He was another family's descendant on my lands. That was how he and Ann had met. They'd been childhood sweethearts. He would be changing, too. Fuck, I hoped he stayed hidden and safe.

"Tara, go make sure the kids are okay," I directed.

She scoffed, and I automatically curled my lips and slapped my fist on the counter warningly. She was always dismissive with them, and I'd never cared for it, but I preferred to ignore it. Now, however, I wouldn't let the disrespect go.

It was as if I'd been half a person this entire time. Half asleep.

Tara moved out of the room quickly, shooting me a fearful look from the corner of her eyes.

"Ann," I began, and the small wolf's ears flattened as her tail lowered with fear. "Can you change back?"

She whimpered in answer. I was going to have to force her, which was what I didn't want to do. Forcing always hurt more. I remembered when I'd changed for the first time. The tugging and pulling of muscles and limbs reforming was jarring, but you eventually got used to it. Even craved the pain of the change.

"Change back," I ordered, infusing power into my tone. The kind that only alphas were able to use.

Bones creaked and muscles moved as she went through the change. There were two stages. One was when we were fully a wolf and the other was the midway change, but only the strongest were able to half shift.

Once she was finished, Ann curled on the cold ground. I gripped the blanket on the couch and spread it over her.

"I never thought this would happen in my lifetime." She shuddered with a sob. I patted her back awkwardly. Restless energy filtered through my body. It was an urge to find Boots. I tried to focus on my packmate as she cried.

"You'll be fine." I softened my tone. "Lawrence will be home soon."

I counted everyone that would change into wolves on my land. They needed guidance and help from their alpha right now, not have him run off half-cocked to the little fae he had a hard-on for. I ground my molars as the heaviness on my shoulders compounded.

I traded a look with Daniel and his head dipped in deference, waiting for my orders.

I had an obligation to help my people, but as soon as I was done, that fae ass was mine. No one ran away from me—she was mine.

For now.

CHAPTER 20
CAMILLA

Parking that monster of a truck was something I never wanted to repeat. I was so crooked, it wasn't even funny. Who even needed a truck that big?

I didn't let myself stress about it, though. I was sure all the cops were too busy putting out figurative fires all over town. I'd seen about twelve police cars zooming around in different locations. There must be crazy shit going down. The last thing they were going to worry about was how I was parked.

I hopped up the steps of my townhouse and lifted my hand to knock. When no one appeared at my fifth knock, I tried the door. Surprisingly enough, it opened.

Thea and Rosalind must not be home, then. They were sticklers for locked doors. I kicked the door shut behind me and stepped through.

"Rosalind, Thea, Eliza?" I called out all my roommates' names. There was a crash from the kitchen, and I ran toward the alarming noise.

Eliza was on the ground, her head bent.

I gasped at the spilled water and shattered glass. She was

using her hands to brush all the broken stuff together. "Where's Mr. Fins?"

Eliza lifted tortured eyes to me and wailed, "I killed him!"

Uh, oh.

She was heading into meltdown mode. I needed to calm her down before she got hysterical.

Once, she'd gone full-blown crazy mode on me. I shivered at the memory. For such a levelheaded, self-proclaimed pessimist, she had a fountain of emotions bottled.

My boots crunched over the glass, and I grabbed her arm and pulled at her. Suddenly, she was standing, and I stumbled back.

My mouth dropped at her quick motion. Her hands were wet with water and mingled with a purple substance that looked a lot like blood.

I gripped her hand and lifted it closer to my face. She had multiple gashes on her hands that seeped purple blood, and little slivers of glass were embedded in her skin.

Fae bled purple.

I'd seen it before, but out of sight, out of mind.

Seeing it come out of my bestie was a trip. Rae really had freed magic.

Eliza glanced down, and her face twisted.

"Take deep breaths," I ordered. "I don't think it'll be good for you if you heal with glass in you."

I corralled her to the couch and went to grab my tweezers and a dish. Once I'd retrieved them, I settled onto the couch next to her. She looked different in the artificial light of the living room. I was able to see her clearly for the first time. Her red hair was more vibrant than usual, deeper in color. The lush locks were tight rings.

Wracking my brain for a topic to distract her with, I said the first thing that popped into my head. "What happened to Fins?"

"I was holding his bowl when all of a sudden this whoosh came over me. My stomach twisted, and I felt all sorts of things." She shivered. "It's hard to explain."

I bet. If I had felt a chill and the hair raise on my arms, I couldn't imagine what *actually* changing did.

Or maturing—that was what Unnaturals called it. I struggled to wrap my mind around this other species thing. A species that I was now positive I would join when I turn twenty-two in a few days.

Realization struck me.

That's why the cops were all over the place. The Unnatural community had exploded. I imagined various scenarios. People going out, families having dinner, being on a date, and then changing into something you had no idea of.

The fear, the confusion. At least Eliza had known what her change meant, but not everyone did.

"So you dropped his bowl?" I prompted.

Eliza nodded frantically. I'd never seen her this upset. She usually took everything in stride, almost like she was numb to the surprises in life. It had to do with her porn star mom, but she'd never told me more than that.

"When I came out of my blackout, I saw him flop his last flop, and I rushed to grab him." She shuddered and sobbed. "And he popped in my hand!" The wails began again. "I"—she hiccupped—"flushed him."

I imagined a squashed fish, and my stomach heaved a bit.

"Hey, stop that now," I said softly, gripping her shoulder. "Things happen. You told me that. Might as well go with it. It could have been worse, right?" I cleared my throat. I was just using her mindset against her. "I mean, it could have been a human, right?"

Eliza slumped into the couch.

"We'll go buy a Fins number two," I offered, and she perked up a bit. She had this thing with routine, and feeding the angelfish was part of it. "I'll get changed and we can head out, and I can fill you in on my second kidnapping."

"What?" she yelled and shot to her feet so fast I got dizzy.

"Yeah, you remember that sexy man from the bar?" My tone seeped with bitterness. "He was a fucking werewolf staking out Rae. Those drinks they sent us that tasted so good had wolfsbane, and I guess fae react a certain way to it."

Eliza's eyes were so wide I was about to ask her to blink before they rolled out of her head. Her gaze narrowed.

"Oh, shit, you slept with him, didn't you?" I pressed my lips together, nodding as she fell back into the couch dramatically. "Camilla bagged a werewolf," she muttered disbelievingly, shaking her head. Rolling my eyes, I plucked the last glass shard from her palm. "Oww!"

I grabbed the wet towel and pressed it to her hand. When I pulled it away, I saw the small gashes beginning to slowly mend.

Weird, yet cool.

"And he was magnificent. Werewolves may be my new flavor," I claimed, wiggling my eyebrow at her, trying to make light of it even though my chest stung in betrayal.

He'd looked me in the face and lied about Tara, not once, but twice.

I'd had enough of his goddamned bullshit.

"Are you sure that would be a good idea? I mean, isn't sleeping with them dangerous?"

"You want me to serial date and not allow anything juicy to happen?" I rolled my eyes. I didn't have an extensive sex filled past, but at least I wasn't scared of my sexuality.

Sometimes Eliza gave me the vibe that she was. Not that I jumped into every bed I came across, but I'd had a handful of lovers. As long as the attraction was there, I was game. Thing was, it didn't happen often.

"I'm selective, is all," Eliza snapped.

"His bedroom skills are beside the point. Greyson's bad news and a liar. I feel a little like a hoe. He had a girl who lives in his house and everything. I mean, she was a total bitch. She even tortured me. Like, legitimately beat the crap out of me." I peered over Eliza calculatingly. "Maybe you can kick her ass for me?" My accent thickened with my anger.

"I can hold her down while you kick her face in," she offered. I grinned at her words. "Is that where the bruises are from?" Right, the yellowing bruises across my cheek. At least the one on my forehead had faded so it was barely a discoloration. "I was waiting for you to mention them, but you were taking too long," she admitted.

I set the bowl and tweezers aside. "Yep, it was her."

My phone rang, startling me. I pulled it out of my shorts and answered the unknown number.

"Howdy, Camilla here."

"Camilla," Greyson's voice filled the speaker, and a shiver slipped down my spine.

I met Eliza's eyes, and her eyebrow twitched up as she tilted her head. "What do you want?"

"Get back here."

"Uh, no," I said slowly. Did he really think that would work? "But thanks." A rough growl vibrated my cell. Eliza fanned her face as I tried to stifle the need he inspired. "Is that all? I have some errands to run."

"Wait, where are you going? Don't go outside—"

"Okay, bye," I chirped and hung up.

"Um, if that's his voice, I can see why you couldn't help yourself."

"I know, right? Even you would have given into his wolfish charms," I said, even the thought of Greyson giving his charms to someone else made my temper bubble. I pushed that thought away and stood. "Do you like the hooch ass shorts I stole?" I wiggled my bottom. The hem grazed just below my ass.

Eliza snorted. "They pair especially well with the boots."

I rolled my eyes at her. The ensemble did make my profession questionable. Not that I had a profession at the moment considering I was living on my savings and I regretted the degree I'd chosen.

"I'm going to go get in some of my own clothes and then we can head out to the pet store before they close," I said. Eliza's smile slipped, and I could tell she didn't want to be alone. I squeezed her shoulder. "I won't be long."

She inclined her head, and I sped to my bedroom for a quick shower and to get out of Tara's clothes.

As soon as I got the chance, I was burning them.

CHAPTER 21
CAMILLA

I STRUTTED DOWNSTAIRS IN JEANS AND A T-SHIRT. No button-down nonsense. That was just another reason I was having a difficult time wrapping my head around actually joining the workforce. I hated dressing professionally. I was sure it had to do with growing up on a farm and the daily manual labor.

"Ready," I called, and Eliza popped up in front of me with a quickness that startled me. "*My goodness*, Eliza, you scared me."

She smiled and practically vibrated with energy. She'd brushed her hair into a tight bun. It was interesting to see someone who liked to make dirty jokes dress so conservatively. Rosalind was the shy one, but even she wore clothing that was more hip-hugging than Eliza did.

"Let's take the wolf's truck," I claimed and wiggled my eyebrow. Eliza grinned and pumped her fist. We locked the door behind us and made our way to the massive, badly parked vehicle.

Eliza cackled. "And you judge my driving?"

Ignoring her, I jumped into the car. The door slammed a

little too hard on her side, and she winced. I noted the uncomfortable look that flashed across her face.

"What's wrong?" My eyebrows furrowed.

"Uh, you know that *thing* Rian told us about, the whole being horny when we mature?" I nodded slowly, thinking back to the tall, good-looking fae who had helped me and the other girls escape Faerie. "Well, he wasn't joking."

She wiggled into the seat and I snorted.

"Looks like you'll have to invest in a vibrator."

"Real talk," Eliza agreed.

"Yes, sex store trip," I yelled. Eliza grinned and turned on the stereo. "Did you think this is where you would be two years ago?"

"You mean, did I think I would have been captured and find out this whole-ass other world existed? No. To put the cherry on the top, I turn out to be one of those creatures that should have been fictional." Eliza huffed with her shoulders slumped. "I'd always known I had bad luck, but damn."

"At least we're not going through it alone," I said and offered a half-smile.

I was closer to Eliza than I'd ever been to anyone else. I'd never had a girl friend before her. It really drove in the fact that all my past friendships were superficial.

Turning the wheel, I sped out of the lot and made my way to the pet store.

"Speaking of, send a check-in message to everyone," I said, thinking about the girls already old enough to have gone through maturity like Eliza.

Eliza reached for her phone. "Thea texted me."

"What did she say?"

"That she changed while she was with Colt. She said to let

her know when you turned up, too," she said as she typed, probably doing exactly that.

"We need to warn Rosalind that she'll change. She probably has no idea all this craziness that's happened. She's all alone up at her family home."

"I'll call." Eliza swiped, and shortly after, the automated voice directed us to the voicemail. "Shit."

"She did say there was spotty reception up there," I said reassuringly. "Don't forget to message Selina and Jasmine."

They took days to answer when any of us messaged, but as much as they tried to run from that fact they were still a part of us. We weren't leaving anyone behind.

Silence filled the car as I moved into a turning lane and waited for the light to switch.

"It feels so weird, Cam. I feel like myself, but I don't know. It's like I have tons of energy." She reached forward and gripped the dashboard.

When I took the turn into the parking lot too hard, something popped, and I scanned the dash where she'd snatched back her hands. There was a dent in the formerly smooth surface. I gaped at the spot.

"Ohmygod, I'm sorry," she cried, her words running together.

"Not my car," I reassured her, but bit back a curse. Greyson was going to be livid. I pressed my lips together.

Who cared if he was? That was what insurance was for.

Pulling into a parking spot with the same finesse as earlier, I shut off the engine.

"We're here," I sang and jumped out of the car. The store name was illuminated except for the last letter, which flickered. I pressed the lock button to the car as Eliza came up next to me. The last thing I needed was for the truck to get stolen.

The door jingled when I pushed it open, and the white linoleum floor reflected the beams on the ceiling. I curled my arm through Eliza's and guided her to the aquarium aisle.

"What are you thinking?" I said, taking in the array of fish. "There's that cute Dory-looking one if you want to change it up?"

She hummed in deep concentration and then tensed. She went so still that it freaked me out a little. Then Eliza pressed a hand into my forearm almost warningly. She leaned close to my ear. "I think we're being watched . . . Ok, I'm sure we're being watched."

I tensed and followed the direction of her gaze to a tall, thin man. He was well-dressed in slacks. His dark shirt gaped open at the top, exposing more of his pale flesh. Oh, and he was beautiful.

His lips widened, and he pushed off the wall. The urge to run hit me square in the chest.

When he was a few feet away, his head canted, and his eyes widened. "Fae," he hissed and flashed sharp fangs at Eliza.

My heart dropped, and adrenaline made my fingertips tingle. "Time to go."

I grabbed Eliza's hand, but I was jerked back as a cold hand wrapped around my arm. I cried out and heard Eliza yell my name as she gripped my shirt.

In the next second, Eliza lifted her foot and kicked him in the stomach. The guy went flying backward.

Eliza gasped at the explosion of glass. Fish spilled onto the ground and flopped on the floor. When she stepped forward to save them, I wrapped my hands around her arms.

My feet slipped under me as she moved forward and dragged me without effort.

"We have to go." I grunted and tried to pull her back. Eliza snapped out of it and let me guide her. She was probably still in shock about all the flopping at our feet. I guided her down the aisle and then a second.

At the third row, I pressed my hand to my mouth as we froze. A man was crouched over a woman, his face buried in her neck with his eyes closed shut. A slight slurping sounded and crimson leaked from the corner of his mouth.

I'd thought we'd been dealing with vampires, but now it was confirmed. No wonder it was so quiet when we walked in.

We hurried backward, and I almost tripped in my haste. A crash sounded from the direction we left the first guy.

"Ben!" the vampire yelled from the fish aisle. "There's a fae in here. Let's kill it. I'll block the door while you find her."

My stomach dropped, and I forced Eliza down the next aisle. The vet clinic counter was at the end, and I headed toward it, tugging her to crouch behind it with me.

I stifled my cry when I saw the man on the floor. His gray employee shirt was soaked with blood, and his pale throat was ripped out. I elbowed Eliza to catch her attention and had to rub my arm at the ache.

I pressed my hand to her mouth before she made a noise and called attention to us.

"We need to get out of here. Do you think you can run out of here carrying me?" I said as quietly as I could. Eliza was still staring blankly. I shook her shoulders, and she nodded rapidly. "Good."

As she wrapped her arms around me, a cold hand gripped me again and tossed me to the side. I skidded across the floor and hit the edge of the metal frame of the aisle. For a second, I couldn't move, the pain flaring up my side keeping me in place.

Groaning, I finally pushed up and found the vampire, Ben, holding Eliza down, gripping her head. His face was smeared with blood. The other clean-cut vampire stood in front of her. I wracked my brain to get their attention off Eliza.

"Hey, morons? You're exposing yourselves. Everyone will know about vampires."

Clean-cut turned in my direction with his lips curled into a sinister smile. "We disabled the cameras." His grin widened. "It looks like the fun can begin. I'll find iron."

"We can rip her head off," Ben said, his savage grin made scarier by the blood around his mouth.

"Wonderful idea. Hold her still," Clean-cut said as he drew his leg back and kicked her side. Eliza grunted in pain and tried to curl into herself, but Ben held her still.

In a swift movement, he punched her face, and blood burst all over the place.

"No," I cried and charged at Ben. I landed on his back, and he turned, gripping my neck.

"You're nothing, weak little human." His teeth gleamed, and my short life flashed in the back of my head.

The oddest part was that Greyson's face flickered before my eyes as the vampire leaned toward my neck.

CHAPTER 22
GREYSON

Rage wasn't a new concept for me. But when I saw that vampire wrap its hands around Camilla's neck, wrath unlike anything I'd ever known seeped into my blood so potently that I could taste it.

I burst into my wolf and ran at the vampire about to sink his teeth into Boots' neck.

In an instant, my sharp teeth hooked into the hard flesh, and I shook my head until he released her. Camilla crumpled to the ground in a pile.

As soon as she was free of his hold, I lunged at his throat and clamped my teeth around the vulnerable flesh. I twisted my head back and forth in hard tugs, using every bit of my Unnatural strength. Skin stretched and tore. When it burst open, salty blood slipped into my mouth.

Daniel was in the middle of dealing with the other vampire, who still tried to claw away, but to no avail. He settled his weight into the vampire's back, nails clawing.

The vampire twisted and kicked back, and Daniel's grip loosened. The bloodsucker got free and tore away before I could grab him. The urge to give chase prickled, but there was one person who held me back. Camilla.

We were lucky to have caught them unaware, so we could mete out their deaths quickly. Otherwise, it would have been drawn out and bloody. Potentially even fatal considering we were even in number.

The redheaded woman fell to the ground and curled her arms around her legs. My eyes narrowed at the purple blood splattered on her face. Daniel caught it at the same time and growled, readying to attack. Camilla stood and shoved past me and ran at the girl.

Upon closer inspection, I recognized her from the bar. Camilla had lied. The other girls with her had probably all been half-breeds.

I growled low, and Daniel stopped stalking the fae girl. I pushed into my human skin and stood. Camilla still hadn't turned as she knelt and hugged her friend tightly.

"Daniel," I barked, unreasonably angry that Camilla hadn't paid attention to me. "I'm going to disable the cameras."

There couldn't be any proof of our existence. As a whole, the community of Unnaturals understood that.

"Those vampires already have," Camilla said, helping her friend off the ground. Her voice was surprisingly steady, and when she turned to look at me, there wasn't any of the shock I expected.

I approached her. "Good. Let's go."

Her eyes flickered to my stiff dick, and my brow lifted when she licked her lips. My cock twitched at her lust filled attention. Her friend leaned close to her and narrowed her eyes at me.

"Damn girl," she whispered. I full-on grinned. Daniel paced, impatient as ever.

"I know, right?" Camilla said. The corner of her lips tilted up, but there was something in her eyes that I didn't fully understand.

Was she . . . jealous? My eyebrows rose further.

"Let's go," I snapped, surprised at the pleasure from the idea of her envy.

"No," she answered crisply. Rage must have contorted my face because she hurried to explain. "We're grateful that you saved our lives, but there's no need for me to come back. I left you my number so you could call me if you need my blood."

Fuck. She was poking holes in my story.

"You won't be any good to me if you're killed before then." Her mouth dropped in indignation. Before she started her anger-fused rant, I continued. "Don't you see? You'll be a target. Fae are hated by all in the Unnatural world." I saw her look toward the exit. She was probably thinking about the vampire.

"You're useless against attacks. Both of you." I used the fear in her eyes. The fact that fae were hated wasn't a lie, but I needed it to seem dire enough for her to realize she needed to come with us.

She pressed her lips together, eyes flashing with indecision. "I won't go without Eliza," she claimed, gripping the fae's hand.

My lip curled, an outright refusal on the tip of my tongue. But then I realized I could use Eliza, who was already a fae. If Tristin needed one . . . I may not have to give up Camilla—I stopped that train of thought right then and there.

Eyeing the fae, I recognized a confused girl who wasn't a threat. I could use her to keep Camilla in line.

"Fine," I said begrudgingly.

Daniel whimpered and kept pacing. I inclined my head for

them to go ahead. Daniel stepped up beside me, anger in his eyes. I narrowed my eyes at him, and he lowered his head, accepting my decision.

Considering Daniel was not only my friend but also my beta, I could count on him to keep me in line, but I knew what I was doing.

I rolled my shoulders. The last couple of hours were intense. Pack issues ate up my time. Most of it was spent reassuring those who had never shifted before in addition to figuring out logistics of child care while parents wrapped their heads around the changes.

Daniel had helped me, but the entire time I couldn't get rid of the looming desire to see Camilla.

I chalked it up to the fear that she was going to run off, and my only lead to fae would disappear. I'd kept one eye on my alpha duties and another on the tracker.

When she started to move from the location she'd been at for a while, I couldn't hold myself back anymore. I took off with Daniel in his sports car and left Ann and Tara in charge. To say I was surprised that the address led me to a pet store was putting it mildly.

Near the store entrance, I dipped down to grab the ripped jeans from my quick shift and fished out the keys to Daniel's car. When I reached my truck, I eyed it to make sure she hadn't crashed into anything, then I held out my hand toward Camilla.

"Give me my keys."

She rolled her eyes, and my cock hardened. Contrary minx. She cleared her throat and fixed her eyes on my chin. By the pink flushing her face, she was checking out the effect of her presence. I stifled my grin.

"Can your friend drive?" I asked and opened my door. I was

going to need to start bringing extra clothes with me. I'd gotten out of the habit.

At Camilla's affirmative, I handed Eliza Daniel's car keys. Daniel growled.

"You ready to change back?" At his silence, I arched an eyebrow. "Go with the girl." He chuffed, disgruntled. "Follow behind me," I ordered Eliza.

"What? Why do we have to go separately?" Camilla gripped Eliza harder.

"Because I don't want you driving my truck, and Daniel doesn't have opposable thumbs."

"I don't like it," Camilla said stubbornly.

I forced myself not to take a step close to her and instead stared her down. "You want your little fae friend to come with me?" I said in a threatening voice.

Camilla's face tightened as she reconsidered. She must have thought Daniel was the lesser evil because she turned to Eliza. "You'll be okay?"

"Don't worry about me." Eliza took a deep breath, and a smile twitched her lips. "I'm getting over my shock. I can handle myself."

With a last hug, Camilla and Eliza separated. Daniel eyed her and walked to the Aston. I climbed in, glad Camilla was already buckling herself in the passenger seat. When I looked up, I gaped at the dashboard. The smooth surface was dented.

"What did you do to my truck?" I roared.

Camilla jumped but was quickly on the defense. "Nothing!" she yelled right back.

I waved a hand at the imperfection. "That's not nothing."

She rolled her eyes. "Stop being a baby."

That almost sent me over the edge, and I growled, jamming

the key into the ignition. "If I was human, you would have killed me of high blood pressure already."

"Well, thank goodness you're immortal."

My teeth clicked together at her sarcasm.

What was even sicker? My cock twitched in response to her attitude. I wanted to pull over, slam her on the hood, and fuck the sassiness out of her.

I steamed in my anger and revved out of the parking lot. She made it more agonizing by casually lifting her boot off the floor and setting it on the bent dashboard. Half the trip went on in silence as I battled the instinct to take her.

I thought about just careening to a stop on the side of the dark road, like that first night when she sucked me off with her pretty, talented mouth. But this time, I'd make sure she was thoroughly fucked.

The mental image of pounding into her silky pussy made me shiver. The truck would rock with how hard I took her . . .

My forehead creased in a frown. Despite what ran in her veins, she was still fragile.

I was able to distance the fact that she was fae enough for my conscience to be okay with being with her. That wouldn't be the case once she turned completely.

"Why do vampires make such a mess by tearing throats out?" she asked out of the blue.

I forced my thoughts away from my lust and worked to make sense of her words. I cleared my throat.

"Not all vampires do. When they do, it's to hide their existence. It makes it look like a wild animal attack."

Understanding and disgust flashed across her features. I turned down the long road to my house. The car behind me sped up, bouncing over the small potholes in the road that were easy for my truck to navigate, but not for the lower build of the Aston. Daniel must be going crazy right now with how that woman guided the car over the rough terrain.

I pulled into my drive minutes later. "Don't step out yet," I ordered and put the car in park. I opened it and listened. Newly matured Unnaturals in shock were dangerous, and there were plenty of those tonight. Especially those who had never turned. That wasn't considering the werewolves as old as me who hated fae for binding magic.

I thought to the packmates who had left to live a human life so long ago. Their descendants were changed now as well. I rubbed my face. There was so much to deal with.

CHAPTER 23
CAMILLA

I IGNORED GREYSON'S OBNOXIOUS ORDER AND stepped next to him. He glared balefully at me, but I shrugged it off as the car Eliza was driving skidded to a jolting halt next to the truck. I winced. It was no secret that my friend was an awful driver.

Eliza's lips curled with anger as she slammed the door shut. I was surprised it didn't fall off. I bit my tongue so I didn't comment on her driving. I'd never seen her so pissed off. My eyebrows flew up when the passenger door slammed open, and Daniel's defined, naked body made a showing. Wow. I was sure Eliza had some choice thoughts about his nudity.

I glanced at Greyson when a growl slipped from his lips. "I thought you weren't switching back for a while."

"That was before you had this fae—" he blustered and paused, searching for a word. "*Woman* drive my car when she doesn't know how to drive." Daniel sneered at Eliza, who flipped him the bird.

"I was already driving, I wasn't going to pull over just because you were throwing a fit," Eliza snapped, her hands clenched at her side. I pressed my lips together as I realized they reminded me of children fighting in the schoolyard.

"You little—" Daniel took a threatening step toward her, looking like he was going to throttle her.

"Try it, dog," Eliza hissed, and I couldn't hold back my laughter at that.

Perfect come back, Eliza.

"Run off the anger," Greyson ordered. Daniel's jaw worked and his eyes flashed. "Check in on the wolves running through the property and see if anyone needs anything. And spread the word to keep away from the main house."

Seconds ticked by before he shifted and took off toward the woods. Greyson muttered something under his breath and climbed the steps of his house. I snapped to get Eliza's attention, which was still attached in the direction Daniel had disappeared. She was definitely fuming.

Eliza caught up to me. She rubbed her forehead and pinched the bridge of her nose.

"You need rest." I grabbed her arm and had a difficult time tugging her. Right, she was stronger than me by a ton. She followed after me as I guided her to the stairs.

"Camilla," Greyson called. I looked down at the foyer and waited for him to continue. "Come down when you settle"— his eyes flicked to Eliza dismissively—"her in."

"I was already planning on it," I snapped and narrowed my eyes at him. I had so much I had to say to him that bubbled under my skin. I'd never been one to hold in what I thought, and I was bursting to get the words out.

I eyed Eliza, who was deep in thought.

Pushing the door to the room I'd been settled in the last

days, I found the plush bedding torn to shreds. I gaped at the massacre. "What happened to the bed?"

Rage bubbled.

I knew exactly who'd done it, and I wanted to wring the bitch's neck. If Greyson hadn't been playing around on her, then she wouldn't have targeted me. *I'd* been the one lied to!

I hated when girls did that.

Take it out on the unfaithful guy, not the unknowing party.

"I'll be back," I said in a clipped tone.

Eliza tossed herself on the bed, and the fuzzy innards of the comforter spread all over the place. "I'll be napping."

I stormed downstairs, hunting for the goddamned dog. Not finding him in the kitchen or living room, I began shoving open the doors.

By the second door, I found him with his back to me. I pushed into the room, and the door clicked shut. He didn't turn around. Instead, he fiddled with some drawers.

"You!" I yelled, anger heightening when he kept ignoring me.

"Do you have something to say?" He finally twisted my way as he threw clothes over his shoulder.

"Yes, I do! You're a shitty person."

"How do you figure?" His lips twitched, and it pissed me off even more. Greyson leaned back as if he was getting ready to hear some magnificent joke.

"You're a liar," I hissed.

Greyson straightened, alarm flashing across his mocking expression, all of a sudden very interested in what I had to say. I ground my teeth together. He was hiding something.

"Your whore-man ways made me a target. You shouldn't have messed around with me if you had a girlfriend, or whatever the hell you guys call each other." The tightness in his shoulders loosened, and his lips twitched. I dug my nails in my palms to keep myself from attacking him. I was no match for a wolf. Greyson's mouth opened as if to speak, but I kept going. "I don't know how you wolves work, but I don't play by those games. I'm here so that Eliza and I can figure out our next steps."

"I—" Greyson started, his face reddening and anger furrowing his brows.

"Also, I would like you to keep that wolf bitch off my back," I interrupted him again. I was getting ready to ask about the Cory situation when he blew up.

"Let me fucking get a word in edgewise. Tara and I are not together," he yelled, and I narrowed my eyes at him. "Yes, she has boundary issues, but we are not whatever you think we are. I have made it clear repeatedly." Greyson strode toward me and gazed down at me.

I shuffled from foot to foot, anxious at his proximity and liking it way too much at the same time. "Bull*shit*," I sneered.

Greyson gripped my chin, a snarl twisting his lips. I should have been terrified, but fear was the furthest thing from my mind. I wanted to wrap myself around him, but only after he fucked me on that bed.

"Okay, I may have kept out that she scratched an itch when it was convenient, but that's it." His hands slashed out in a harsh movement, driving in his point.

I scoffed, but before I could say anything, his lips slammed onto mine. I gave myself over to the punishing twist of his tongue before I snapped out of my lust-induced haze and shoved him back. "I don't get you! You push me away, you draw me back in, and the next second you're going on about hating what I am. Make up your goddamned mind!" I yelled.

He jolted at my volume.

I didn't think I'd yelled that hard since I'd fought with my parents when I was in high school. But my anger melted away just as suddenly as it came. His jaw worked, and I forced myself not to sway toward him.

"No." I released a heavy breath. "No need. I'm done with this back and forth. I wasn't asking for anything deep. You were the one thinking I'm over here wanting more."

My chest tightened. Although I hadn't asked for it, some odd part of me hoped for it.

I turned on the heels of my boots. His heavy hand landed on my arm, and he forced me toward him. The look in his eyes was pure conflict as it battled between lust and hate.

He must have settled on what to feel because he pulled me tight to him. My back bowed as every inch of my body touched his.

"Tara and I are nothing. I should have made sure she left you alone." That was definitely not an apology. It was almost as if he was trying to convey his regret without saying it.

"Why are you explaining it to me?" I didn't understand what was going on between us, and it was tying me up in knots.

He scrubbed his fingers through his hair in agitation.

"I don't know. Despite myself, I find the idea of you seeing me in a negative light repulsive."

"Golly, so romantic," I said. "Every girl loves hearing about being liked despite a man's best efforts"

Greyson's lips tightened, and guilt flashed across his expression. With a heavy sigh, he groaned.

"I'm not great with words."

"Tell me about it," I muttered sarcastically. I was astounded that he was finally saying what he actually felt. He was always on the defensive, but this hint at his true thoughts got to me more than I'd like to admit.

"I want you. I'd never been this drawn to anyone, and I've been alive for a long time." A long time meant many women.

Jealousy stung like an angry hornet, but I pushed that away. As much as I wanted to, I also didn't ask for his body count.

"So, what would this be anyway?" I made myself ask. I wanted to have the lines clearly drawn because I wasn't stepping over it once it was.

"I'm tired of fighting my attraction for you, but nothing serious can happen between us."

"Got it, you have a mate in your future that isn't me," I responded bitterly.

"Exactly," he said curtly. I hated the hurt that caused me. "But I want you. No, I need you. When you ran—" He broke off and inhaled sharply. "When you ran, all I wanted was to hunt you down. Don't ever run from me again." His eyes flashed brighter, and he clutched me tighter to him.

My breasts grew heavy with the need for his mouth. I wanted him all over me. I wanted him behind me.

I craved him just as much as he claimed to want me, but a part of his comment rubbed me the wrong way.

"When I mature, I'll have a mate, too," I muttered to myself.

In the next instant, a vicious growl escaped his lips. He picked me up and slammed me against the wall. Air exploded from my lungs.

Thankfully, it wasn't so hard that he made me go splat. But

the plaster to the side of my head was not as lucky when he drove his fist through the wall.

I gaped at him.

Plaster dust settled in a white plume around us. I didn't have time to address whatever that was before he was kissing me again. I gripped the waistband of his jeans as I angled my head to deepen the kiss.

The scent of forest and fresh air clung to him, making me needier. After unbuckling his jeans, I pushed him back and wiggled out of mine, unwilling to have him destroy them. I shucked the panties and shirt, and then we were both naked.

We stilled for a second. His eyes devoured me from head to toe, and I couldn't say it didn't affect me.

I gripped his arm and tugged him to me, lifting my leg to wrap around his waist. He curled another hand under my other leg and pulled it around him until my ankles pressed into his lower back. Our movements were slow and gentle, and it took my breath away. It was a stark contrast to our first time.

Leaning my head back, our eyes met. A world of confusion and lust reflected back at me. I reached up and tugged his head down. The kiss was soft and sweet as he pressed his cock into me, rubbing against my damp pussy.

"God, Boots. You drive me crazy." Greyson groaned and pressed his forehead to mine.

CHAPTER 24
CAMILLA

"Did you just call me Boots?" I asked, trying to stifle my laugh.

Before he could answer, an odd sensation flooded through me, and my skin broke out in goosebumps. With a surprised yelp, I pulled away, and in doing so, I fell to my knees.

"Camilla," he exclaimed, sounding far away.

I curled into myself. The sharpest pain speared through me, as if little pieces of glass traveled within my bloodstream. I must have blacked out for a second because when I came around, I was fully spread out on the ground.

"What happened?" I groaned and clasped my head.

Greyson's breathing sounded louder than I'd ever heard it, as if his heart rate was elevated. I focused on that slight sound. His heart *was* racing.

Just as I thought about pushing myself up off the ground, I was suddenly sitting. My head spun from how fast I moved, and I threw out a hand to steady myself.

"You've matured," he said almost grimly.

I blinked at him. He was a few feet away from me, his body

angled half toward me. "You're going to turn tail and run now that I changed," I said and couldn't help the regret in my words.

I eyed his stiff body and the still erect cock between his legs. I licked my lips as thoughts that should have been the furthest thing from my mind came to the forefront. I clenched my legs together as I grew wet.

My nose flared, and I realized I could sense my need. His eyes flashed, telling me he knew how wet I was, too.

Self-loathing reflected in his eyes. "I should."

"Bye," I snapped and pushed to stand. Suddenly, I was once again plastered against the wall.

"I said, I should. Not that I was." Greyson nibbled up my jaw. I whimpered, feeling each graze clenching low in my gut.

Everything was magnified. Every touch, graze, and lick was sharp with my newly sensitive skin.

"Get inside me," I ordered and gripped his neck to jump up and wrap my legs around his waist, moving smoother with my new strength.

While it took some effort and some help from him as a human, this time, I was able to balance myself on my own.

I angled up and felt him at my entrance before I slammed myself down. I cried out as the sharpest pleasure rushed through me. It was like two pieces coming together.

I felt right.

Whole.

Greyson stilled and tensed inside me.

He snarled, skin undulating and muscles bulging. I pulled back, mouth dropping at the fullness of him inside me. His cock swelled even more, and we froze, stuck together as my body adjusted to the painful thickness.

I met his eyes. Complete shock stared back at me. His face

sharpened like it had when he was about to shift. Fur sprouted down his neck and back of his hands, and his body grew. The hands gripping my ass tensed.

He pulled one hand away from my ass and reached for my face. I eyed the sharp wolf-like claws near my chin. He carefully clasped my jaw, his nails gentle against my face. Tenderness filled his expression as he leaned close to me.

My tongue curled in his mouth, and I felt the rasp of a sharp tooth. Before I became alarmed, he thrust and sent shivers over my skin.

He withdrew, leaving me feeling empty before feeding himself inside me once again. At the base of his cock, the fullness returned, and I gasped, my head falling back. He pushed the rest of the delicious fullness in me, locking us together. He did that slow thrust again, and this time I expected the extra swelling. *His wolf's knot.*

"Harder," I panted.

Greyson growled and did as I ordered, burying his face in my neck. He pounded into me in earnest. The rhythmic smack of him ramming into me echoed. My moan was loud—wild. I trailed my hands over his shoulder and down his back.

Desperate, I dug my fingernails into his chest, bucking to urge him faster.

Plaster cracked at my back, but other than a slight soreness, it wasn't anything I couldn't handle.

His teeth pressed into my sensitive neck, hard. Moisture leaked from my core, my channel clutching him. I sank my nails into his skin, whimpering. He sank his teeth deeper and it catapulted me into an intense, eye-crossing release. My pussy clenched around him, clasping him in rhythmic jerks.

Stars burst behind my eyelids, and my jaw slackened as he violently slammed into me, making my lower back hit the wall.

Another wave built, and I craned my neck, needing his teeth inside me.

Greyson needed no other encouragement. He struck, sinking his teeth into my neck. He bit down hard. I bucked against him wildly, completely lost to him as I fell into another climax.

I blacked out from pleasure.

He stilled deep inside me, holding me in place with his teeth. His cock jerked in my channel in sharp tugs. Liquid leaked down my thighs—a mix of both our releases. Greyson's teeth detached from my neck with a groan. He licked the wound, once twice and then lifted to kiss me hard enough for my tooth to sink into his lip. The taste of copper spread on my tongue. Heat spilled through my veins, heightening at my wrist, but I couldn't tear myself off his lips. His knot had painfully swelled inside me. I tried to move to lessen the pressure, but literally could not. My legs limply slipped down his waist. He was the only thing holding me up.

Silence descended as we huffed against each other. I finally got my sea legs under control. Catching my breath, I touched my neck and drew my hand away. Purple blood.

"That was probably the craziest sex I've ever had." I huffed out a laugh. "I'm thinking I'll enjoy having sex as a fae." Greyson still hadn't looked at me. He was probably worried that I'd get all attached. Wanting to subtly tell him that I still understood his line, I added, "Maybe I'll try a vampire next."

A sharp, stinging sensation twisted in my stomach.

Jealousy?

"Try?" he spat, so still it was a little scary. Why was he so pissed? I scowled and cleared my throat. Time to get off him before I started getting all fluttery over his jealousy. Gripping his shoulder as a purchase, I yanked myself down, detaching off his knot. Damn, that stung.

"I meant fuck," I spat back just as aggressively as him.

Greyson roared and brought his knuckles into the wall again, making a hole. I gawked up at him.

"You will never touch anyone again," Greyson rasped, his words guttural.

I flattened against the wall.

What the hell was wrong with him? I clutched my stomach, a sick feeling there.

"What in the hell?" I yelled. Feeling all kinds of off, I dipped and grabbed my clothes and got dressed, eyeing his huffing form from the corner of my eyes. "I'll leave you to whatever little meltdown you have going here," I muttered.

A shadow of frustration made me hesitate.

I frowned; I wasn't frustrated though.

What was going on?

Greyson turned and stood before me. He reached for my hands, but I evaded his touch. Hurt rushed through me, and then I realized what was going on.

My eyes widened and I sucked in a breath. Greyson nodded, answering my suspicion.

The emotions were *his*.

"I claimed you. We can feel each other's emotions."

My mouth dropped. "B-but you said we weren't mates. You made that *very* clear."

"I'm sorry," he rasped and tried to reach for my hands again. I felt his frustration. "The idea of cross-species matings are a far-off concept to me. I'd never met anyone that's had a mate of a different species."

"Who gave you permission to claim me!" I was on the verge of hyperventilating. "Tell me how to block this." Even as I said it, I imagined our connection barred up. Like erecting a mental wall. Automatically, there was a bereft sensation that took my breath away. Greyson jerked, and I knew I'd succeeded.

"I understand your caution," he began slowly. "Let me explain."

I scoffed and finished buttoning my jeans, then shoved my feet into my boots. "No thanks. You said this was just fucking. I'm keeping to my side of the line."

I pushed past him. My hand tingled where I touched his chest, and it took a force a will not to shove him back on that bed all over again. I craved that fullness.

Hurrying out of the room, I slammed it behind me harder than I'd intended. I made sure to take measured, calm steps to the bedroom upstairs, where I closed the door behind me and slumped against it.

No, what he was saying . . .

I squeezed my eyes tight.

Camilla, you can't deny the connection.

"So, I was exploring," Eliza said, startling me. "Did I tell you that back at the townhouse I could hear most of what the neighbors were doing if I wasn't focusing on *not* listening in? Well, I couldn't hear anything outside this room. I have a feeling the rooms have soundproofing. Anyway, I digress." I slid into the bed next to her, taking note of her smirk. "There I was, exploring, when I passed this door and the loudest scream I've ever heard slipped through the crack of the door."

"Do you figure the door isn't set right?" I muttered, only

giving her a small percentage of my attention. I was still stuck on what had just happened with Greyson.

My Greyson.

My stomach churned.

Nope, I needed to stay far away from that train of thought. His talk of mates and crap didn't mean I agreed to any of that.

"No sound proofing could have contained that scream." She started choking on her laugh. "I thought someone was killing you. It wasn't until you started chanting *harder* that I ran the other way." She giggled.

I'd been yelling *harder*?

Wow, I must have blanked on that. It was probably in the middle of my orgasm. I'd never experienced anything like that. That full sensation made my toes curl.

I rolled my eyes and nudged her.

"You changed," Eliza gasped. "But you're not twenty-two yet."

I gaped. That was true. There must be something wrong with me.

"Goddammit. I'm going to have to ask Greyson."

"I didn't think you'd have anything against asking him considering what I heard."

"That's if he didn't have some dumb notion that I was his mate," I grumbled.

Eliza eyed me, and I knew what she was thinking. I may not know everything about this world, but I wasn't dumb either. No one ever just randomly felt another person's emotions.

And yes, I was in denial.

CHAPTER 25
GREYSON

I raked my fingers through my wet hair. She was my mate. My fucking mate. All these emotions I'd been battling against and couldn't completely shake were because she was mine.

I laced my fingers behind my neck and kicked the broken bed frame again. As all Unnaturals understood and experienced, when you had a mate, there were no forced feelings. The emotions would be there eventually.

Knowing someone was your mate just made it easier to recognize the one who completed you. And for some, it quickened the process of courtship, less room for stupid irreversible mistakes that way.

For example, if I had known she was mine, I would have never treated her the way I did. I would have never trapped and starved her and belittled her for what she was. I leveled another kick at the bed, and the final leg gave out.

I would have never allowed any harm to come to her.

Cross-species matings were rare. In the years I'd been around, I'd heard of a handful, but had never encountered one.

They weren't common enough for information about how cross-species mates would recognize one another. Many species had different ways of knowing their mates, but there were general rules that followed recognizing each other as long as both parties were of the same species.

Werewolves and many of the other animal Unnaturals never recognized their mates with absolute certainty unless there was sex involved.

Though if I looked carefully, I could have recognized the signs. I'd been obsessive about Boots.

I couldn't get her out of my head, and I'd wanted her more than I'd wanted anything. Even at the expense of my conscience.

All these aspects were out of character for me. Even if they weren't, the intensity of which I felt them should have notified me.

If I'd realized this sooner . . .

The memory of holding her wild little body filled my head. Both times. And fuck, she had taken me deep.

The explosive orgasm sucked the breath from my lungs. I'd never known I could be so sensitive. The knot at the base of my dick wouldn't swell unless I was with my mate, and I was already craving the ecstasy of her taking me with her greedy little pussy. I rubbed the zipper of my jeans where the head of my cock pushed against the seam.

She was mine now.

Wholly mine.

My bite while locked deep inside her had cemented the bond. Our lives were tied together. And I didn't want it any other way.

Even so, at the edge of my conscience swirled guilt. I'd lied to her. If I told her everything—no. I refused to risk our already tumultuous relationship.

My head whipped in the direction of an obnoxious ringing. I strode over to it and answered.

"Greyson," Tristin said from his end.

Dread balled in my stomach. I'd agreed to give my mate over. I'd never asked what they'd do with her either. I hadn't cared to know.

The phone creaked in my hand, but I stopped myself before I cracked it in half.

"What?" I snapped as I mulled over what to say. Camilla was a fae, but now she was a part of me, and I would never give her over.

"We should be there in a few days, I'll message you the location to meet me. Shit." There came cursing on the other end. I strained my hearing. "I'm trying to acquire some more spelled chains for this fae we captured. He's a strong one."

Alarm stemmed through me. I thought of Camilla in that situation, and I wanted to tear out Tristin's throat.

"I have to go. This fucker is slippery." The line went dead.

I paced from wall to wall. We needed a fae, but Camilla wasn't the only fae here. That redhead. I would hand over that one.

It would fulfill my promise and protect Camilla at the same time. I just needed to find a way to separate her friend from her, so she didn't realize what I planned. She wouldn't have to know anything more than her friend had left.

Plans formed, and I considered various options. Both to get the other fae away from Camilla and to soften my mate toward me. She had this look in her eyes when she got me naked . . .

I tugged off my shirt and strode to the kitchen.

THE STEAKS SIZZLED in the pan. I grimaced when I lifted the spoon a little too quickly and the juice of the steak jumped onto my skin. I hadn't really thought this seduction technique through.

Cursing, I rubbed the juice off my chest with a hand towel. The side door leading outside slammed open and then shut.

"Go with pancakes next time," Daniel said, eyeing my naked torso with a smirk. "Are you trying to seduce her with food now? I would have already gotten all the answers I needed out of her by now. You should have left it to me. I would have had her crying out anything I wanted." His eyebrow waggled up and down suggestively.

I wasn't new to Daniel's comments. Never had I thought much of them. I'd actually laughed along with him in every other instance.

Not this time.

My lip curled, and my sight sharpened. Instinct demanded I tear his throat out. Daniel's eyes skidded to the side, not meeting mine.

I slammed my eyes shut, trying to get in control of myself before I attacked my best friend and beta.

When I finally opened them, Daniel was preternaturally still. He understood I was on the brink of attacking him.

"She's my mate," I forced between curled lips. His head lowered.

"A fae?" Daniel said, raking his hands through his hair. He grimaced as if the thought of being mated to a fae was disgusting. "You're fucked."

I would have agreed before Camilla. Shame beat down on me.

I raked a hand through my hair as I thought about my small pack. Before, if I had come home with a mate who was not a wolf, I would have had to leave if I wanted to claim her. There was no known pack mixing.

We had some that married in the human sense with other wolves. Even though we weren't able to have children, we still had companionship until one or both got killed. Or even divorced. The life of an immortal was rough, and while it would be easy for mates to be together forever, it was because they were meant to be. It was unlikely to get tired or divorced from your true mate.

Choosing to be with someone was nothing compared to the relationship between true mates, but it served as a suitable substitute for many wolves.

The tricky thing was if a married wolf ever found their true mate. That was an unpleasant situation I'd only ever witnessed once. I supposed it was a good thing you had to fuck to find out if you truly were mates. As long as you kept it in your pants, the chance went down to zero.

Just as I had brushed away the whirling emotions brought on by Camilla, anyone could convince themselves of the same.

"That's fucking rare. Mixed pups. You won't know whether you'll get a fae or a wolf," Daniel continued. Children. I stilled. It was a possibility for me now that I'd found the only one who could bare me a family. "What if the pack doesn't accept her? I mean, even though pack life isn't the same anymore with magic being gone so long, we still have a hierarchy."

"The pack is small. They live on my land because I protect them. If they want to leave, I won't stop them." I shrugged.

Daniel's eyes flew up and met mine. Alarm shifted through his gaze.

"You'd do that for one of those? You've hated fae for as long as I can remember."

"I was wrong." I shouldn't have held her responsible for things that weren't her fault. Especially my parents' and brother's deaths. I'd always associated fae with the rage of that night, but Camilla wasn't at fault.

Daniel's mouth dropped.

"You're such a prick."

My head turned to find Camilla and Eliza with their arms linked. I hadn't heard the soft fall of footsteps as they'd approached. Eliza leveled her glare on Daniel, anger swirling in her eyes. Mine flashed over to Camilla, who attempted to hide her reaction.

"Fucking dog," Eliza tacked on to her statement.

Daniel gaped at her. He recovered quickly, and his expression smoothed into one of the familiar flirty smiles.

"Now, darlin'." Daniel licked his lips. "I'm more than willing to show you exactly where I want to put my prick."

Eliza held her hand up, disgust on her face, and slid into the chair furthest from him. "Not interested."

I allowed my gaze to trail to Camilla. From the look on her face, she'd heard the end of our conversation. Her brown eyes were lit up with surprise.

Her eyes flicked down to my bare chest, and her nose slightly flared, her pupils dilating. Such a temptation. I forced myself to turn away before I shoved her against the fridge and claimed her again, even with the audience.

"I'm making you dinner," I blurted. Fuck, was I blushing?

"I'm not hungry." Her head tilted to the side. "At all."

The wound at her throat had completely healed with a scar so faint I could hardly see it.

The tongs clattered on the counter when I tossed them. I'd fucking forgotten fae didn't eat. Unnaturals with an animal form always did because it was turned into energy.

I was out of my fucking element.

A soft smile twisted her lips, and she slid into the chair next to her friend. She peeked at me from the corner of her eyes.

Now I had to make sure she never found out I'd lied to her from the start.

CHAPTER 26
CAMILLA

"What?" Eliza sneered, and I found her glaring at Daniel. His eyes flicked away as he returned the glower.

"Stupid fae," he muttered under his breath, but of course, we all heard with our new and improved senses.

I didn't miss the warning look Greyson sent him, and I softened even further. Greyson was so protective; I couldn't function with how turned on that made me.

He'd seemed genuinely upset that I wasn't hungry . . .

It made me almost want to lie to see that sheepish look in his eyes again. I wiggled in my seat and forced my eyes away from his bare shoulders.

Eliza's torso was angled toward Daniel's and his toward hers as they glared at each other. Eliza moved oddly, and I realized she was clenching her thighs together. She'd been struggling with being turned on this entire time. I knew exactly what she meant when she said there was a painful edge to it because I struggled with the same issue.

The desire wasn't made easier with the half-naked man cooking the steaks. It'd built to an uncomfortable level.

Eliza slammed her hand on the island, and I was surprised it didn't crack. Her head bent, and she squeezed her eyes shut. "Can you guys explain the maturity thing?"

Daniel's eyes flared wide, and Greyson cleared his throat before answering, "It's the period after you reach maturity when your hormones are out of control. The only way to make it subside is by—" Greyson paused and searched for a word.

"Fucking constantly," Daniel finished. He watched Eliza's hunched over form with an odd look in his eyes. His tongue flicked out. "You crave touch and sex constantly. It lasts anywhere between six to nine years."

I straightened so quick I was surprised my spine didn't crack.

"No!" Eliza exclaimed in horror. Daniel got up so fast his chair tipped and crashed to the ground.

He stalked out without a backward glance.

"I need to get out of here." Eliza turned to me with a wheeze. "I think I'm going to see about joining Rosalind in her house. The one far, far away from civilization and people."

"I'll go with you," I said without thinking. My heart beat its rejection of that idea.

"No," Greyson barked, startling both of us. I narrowed my eyes at him. He was not about to tell me what to do.

"You have a good reason to stay," Eliza interrupted before I got a word out. She gave me a look. I thought back to the conversation we had in the room. The one where I told her about how he made me feel and how godlike he was in bed. Her eyebrows rose. Her meaning clearly conveyed.

She thought I should explore what was between us. Even if it didn't work out, I would get good sex out of it, which was a must with neediness dogging our every move.

Pursing my lips, I looked back at Greyson. His gaze was leveled on me. It sent shivers of desire to my pussy. I wiggled against the hard surface again.

"You'll need to stop by a sex store," were the words that I pushed from between my teeth.

"Without a doubt," she agreed.

"I can give you a ride tomorrow," Greyson stated. I peeked at him in surprise.

"It's a couple of hours out," Eliza responded, just as surprised.

"Anything for my ma—Camilla." A grimace flashed across his face as if he hadn't meant to say that. A huge smile spread my lips at his words, but I squashed it as soon as it appeared. "I have an errand to run anyway."

Was that my heart melting? Fuck, it was.

What was he doing to me?

Eliza's eyes dropped to his chest, and I saw her throat work to swallow. Possessive anger filled me, and I gripped the edge of the counter and took deep breaths.

"I gotta go." She sprang to her feet and took off upstairs. As soon as she was gone, reason came flooding back, and my shoulders relaxed.

When I looked up, I found Greyson watching me closely, the smallest smile quirking the corner of his mouth.

"Thank you for taking her," I said and turned away, swallowing hard. He really was unlike any guy I'd ever been involved with. I didn't know when I'd stopped comparing him to Jaden.

"Anything for you," he repeated and rounded the corner of the island to push between my legs. I automatically spread without thinking. My core pulsed, wanting him in me. Now.

I licked my lips as he pressed against me, already hard as a rock.

A whimper escaped my lips when his cock throbbed. He gripped my legs and wrapped them around his waist.

Greyson dipped and kissed me softly, swallowing my moan.

My throat knotted with emotion at his tender touch. His hand went up to gently cup my face as he deepened the kiss.

I pulled away, panting against his mouth.

"I'm still not over the whole 'keeping me in your basement and lying to me about Tara' thing." His hand flexed on my jaw.

"I shouldn't have been so—"

"That's not an apology—"

"I'm sorry," he interrupted. "I am truly sorry."

I narrowed my eyes.

"I'll do anything you want me to." He leaned down to lick my lips. "Chain me up in the attic, starve me, whatever you say, I will do."

I laughed.

"Fuck, you're too tempting." His words held a snarl. He snatched me up and into his arms, striding with large, jostling steps. Moments later, I landed on a plush surface. My eyes popped open. I was in his bedroom.

On his bed. With him braced on his arms.

The mattress was now at ground level. I scooted to my elbows. His eyes softened, and he pecked my lips.

"My turn," I whispered, and in a smooth motion, I had him under me. This fae strength and speed were something else. I slid down and jerked his jeans off, accidentally tearing them in the process. I gripped the two ends since they were already ruined and tore them the rest of the way. His cock sprung out.

My tongue flicked out to wet my lower lip, and I looked into his heated gaze.

"This doesn't mean anything," I breathed, not even believing myself.

"Whatever you say," he said with a growl. I dipped and slid my lips past his tip before popping back up and glaring.

"I'm serious," I claimed again, trying to convince myself.

This warm wiggling *feeling* in my chest was foreign.

His head fell back on a groan. Right, I was talking too much. My lips clasped onto his cock, and I bobbed down.

Twirling my tongue, I took him deeper and deeper until he touched the back of my throat. Forcing myself not to gag, I angled my neck in just the right way, and my cheek stretched. I swept my tongue across the underside, and he moaned gutturally. The base of his cock swelled.

Big, bad wolf liked the underside licked. It spurred me on and made my channel spasm with the need to get him inside me.

Lifting my head, I licked my lips and met his eyes. They burned with desire, and a blush warmed my skin.

"You're already so big." My hand wrapped around his hardness, fingertips unable to meet. "You felt like you grew three times this when you were inside me."

"I did," he admitted. My eyebrows furrowed at his comment.

He reached down and gripped my hand and slid it down his cock. I swallowed hard at the sight of his hand engulfing mine as we held his hard length.

"The base expanded when I was inside you. You had to adjust, that's why I couldn't move. It locked us together." By the rasp in his voice, Greyson enjoyed the sight of our hands touching him as much as I did.

"And you don't expand with, uh, others?"

My eyes flicked away from his piercing stare. He definitely knew I was asking out of jealousy.

His thumb brushed my cheek, and he forced me to look at him as he cradled my face. I refused to acknowledge the way I leaned into the touch. I'd never been so vulnerable. My insides were going crazy, and it was because of this werewolf in front of me who claimed we belonged together.

"I have never felt so much pleasure." Honesty reflected in his unclouded green eyes.

A pleased grin escaped before I could stifle it, and I pressed my lips against the tip. He reached up and gripped my hair. He forced my lips to slide down.

Swirling my tongue, I dragged my teeth lightly on his flesh as I retreated. He cursed, and I splayed on his chest a second before he rolled and switched our positions.

Desire licked at me with our bodies pressed so closely together. His weight was pleasantly heavy on top of me. I sighed with relief, tension seeping from my limbs.

My eyes fluttered shut as he nudged at my core, and with a thrust, he speared me and stilled, that same fullness expanded his cock. It wasn't as shocking this time, and it wasn't long before I moved on him, silently asking for more.

And he gave it to me, deepening with every thrust.

I reached a hand between our bodies as he slipped in and out of me, our combined slickness making my fingers slide easily. I gripped his thrusting cock and slid lower to the thick base.

He cursed and gripped my wrist and slammed it onto the

bed, holding it there. My orgasm came in a rush, my channel dragging his out of him with vicious tugs. My limbs became noodles, and I gazed at him as his emotions slipped past my defenses.

Such tenderness . . .

My throat tightened.

"I'm not done," he said with a growl. "I need you to come again."

He slowed his rhythm, my sensitive flesh making me jerk. Greyson leaned down and pressed kisses to my neck.

"Goddammit," I huffed and blinked blearily up at the ceiling as I felt another orgasm build.

CHAPTER 27
CAMILLA

I LAY ON THE LARGE BED CONTENTEDLY. GREYSON was propped on his elbow, staring down at me. His fingers brushed across my lips. He'd been staring at me nonstop. I kept trying to force my eyes away from the unfathomable look in his, but I was drawn back every time.

"I'm sorry I allowed you to be in pain," he finally rasped. I focused on him. His eyes had lowered. My chest squeezed, and I placed my hand on top of his. "And I'm not just saying that because of the mind-blowing sex. I've been sorry from the beginning. I let my prejudices control me."

Craning my neck, I scrutinized my naked skin. I was bruise-free and it was thanks to that fae accelerated healing.

His chest shuddered, but I didn't push him to speak.

"My parents and younger brother were murdered because of my mistakes." He swallowed hard, and I dragged my hand through his hair, listening intently. "I was foolish and rash."

"Why do you think it's your fault?" I murmured.

"I don't think. I know," he said curtly. I flicked an eyebrow up at his tone, and he slumped into the mattress. "Daniel and I were on a night out. We lived up north, closer to Colorado at that point. The community of werewolves was close-knit. We spurned any outsider, but those in our prime liked to go out to the growing cities for entertainment." He flicked a look at me. "We came across a female fae. Daniel and I made a bet to see which of us could get the bitch under us."

I tensed. I wasn't sure what I was more pissed at, him referring to her as a bitch or him wanting to sleep with her. I frowned, and he looked away, expressionless.

"I won," he said bitterly. "But she had a male fae companion. He went crazy. We fucked with him, mocking him of the conquest. He was weak, so I didn't think much of him when we released him after beating the shit out of him. Daniel and I went back to the bar." His chest heaved. "I came home to my parents, brother, and a few packmates, all murdered. Their heads had been cut off. It was a massacre. My brother was hanging on by a thread when I arrived, and he told me it'd been a brown-haired fae. The fae I'd beaten."

Greyson blinked rapidly. "They should have never been able to get past the defenses, but," he shuddered again, "Daniel and I were supposed to be on guard that night. We'd thought nothing of leaving for a little fun. Nothing ever happened," he rasped. "How wrong I was."

Pain and guilt radiated from him, and tears formed in my eyes. I was feeling his guilt and pain through the bond.

It sounded fucked up all around, but that fae didn't have to go on a killing spree. I grimaced. Greyson withdrew, but I gripped his hard arm before he pushed off the bed.

This was why he'd pushed me away so harshly. In his eyes, I

represented an event he wanted to forget, just because of what I was.

"You must have been torn, wanting me when I was going to be fae," I murmured, and his eyes flicked away before he pressed his thumb and pointer finger to his eyes.

"I'm sorry," he repeated. While his visage didn't express any pain, I felt it throughout our bond.

"I understand," I breathed. "But you need to let go of what happened. Never forget them, but you were young. Young and dumb. We all make mistakes."

His eyes fixed on mine. I felt a softer, yet tumultuous emotion whirling in him, but he didn't name what it was, and neither did I. I wasn't ready for that.

I exhaled slowly. This was right between us. I felt like I belonged more than I'd ever belonged anywhere. That's why I'd even left the farm, even though my parents loved me. I'd never felt like a part of the town I grew up in. I'd always felt the odd one out.

Who would have thought home was a person?

Jaden was a blip compared to Greyson. The aching hurt he left was insignificant, because Greyson was the healing balm.

All resentment toward Jaden faded like a bad aftertaste.

Greyson had given me a part of his soul with his confession. I exhaled slowly. I wanted to offer him a hint of mine in exchange.

"I didn't even know this world existed," I began. "I went to school. Pursued a degree in something I had no passion for and lived life—just like any human. My life changed the night I was snatched from the street." Everything from that day flooded back.

The uncertainty, the fear that I was going to be sold into sex trafficking. But it was a different kind of sinister. "I was taken along with two other girls that day. Rosalind and Eliza. This psychopath couple dragged us through Faerie. Those first days were the hardest."

I grimaced and turned my head.

"The only food they gave us was oatmeal. It kept us all alive, but put it in front of us now and we'll all gag. They kept us tied up," I continued after a short pause. "That is why Thea, Rosalind, Eliza, and I are the closest. We were there longer than any of the others."

Greyson's expression was troubled. "How did you escape?"

My smile widened.

"They never counted on one of the last girls they took. That cruel couple I mentioned? The male fell for her. That began to unravel everything." I could tell he was surprised at this part.

Similarly to how I'd felt when I'd seen with my own eyes that the fae male truly cared for Rae.

"Fae are and have always been secretive. That's why I took you. We were looking for the girl that was with you that night. The Queen."

I figured.

"What did you want from her?" I asked.

His expression tightened. "I try my best to figure out my enemies."

"Rae isn't your enemy," I said and cut off what else I was going to say when his eyes flashed to me.

"The antagonism toward fae wasn't only brought on by what happened to my family. Since I was young, the idea that fae were the enemy has been driven in. Not only for me but for most other Unnaturals. It's a truth we live by. It stems from being kicked out of Faerie and stories of the Unnatural world. I, like many others, have never been to Faerie, but that's where we were all created before a fae King forced out most every species after a war the fae started. Unnaturals have reason to hate fae. Our history bleeds because of them."

I scowled. I'd no idea this hostility existed. I'd have to find a way to get word to Rae before she was blindsided by this hate toward her simply because she was the Queen. She was walking into a whole system already against her.

I could see the question in Greyson's eyes. He wanted to ask what I knew, but I smiled with my lips pressed together.

"You said you chose a degree you didn't want?"

I nodded, glad he hadn't asked about Rae, and smiled slightly. "What about you? In your long life, have you gone to college?"

"No, I had to run a business." He winked. "Even immortals need to make money. How do you think I could afford this land?"

"What kind of business?"

"My grandfather started in farming. That got passed down to me from my father, but over the years, I've developed a passion for whiskey. I have distilleries on this land. Some of my pack work there." Greyson grinned, lost in thought. "What about you? What's your passion?"

"I don't know," I responded honestly. "I grew up on a farm in a small town." Shrugging, I cleared my throat. "My adoptive family loves me, but it was strange growing up looking so different from them." I smiled wryly. "I researched the most lucrative career choice and went for it. I told myself that an accounting degree was solid. But now I'm on the other side with said degree, and I dread working."

"Well now you have an eternity to figure it out." His wink made my stomach explode in butterflies. Huh, I guess I did. "And there's nothing that interests you?"

My face reddened. "I liked tending to farm animals." I shrugged and changed the subject. "Speaking of living, how's Cory? Have you gotten word about the witch coming to help heal him with my blood?"

Greyson's eyes flickered, and he tensed, his jaw working overtime.

"She backed out," he said finally, "but I'll begin searching for another way to get him healed. Now that magic has returned, we just have to find a way to keep him alive until he turns."

My shoulders loosened. That sounded promising. There had to be someone who had that type of magic. Rae might know . . .

The bedroom door slammed open, causing me to jolt to the side and thump on the ground. Greyson was already on his feet, growling at the door.

Tara gaped at us. My hands fisted when her eyes swiped over Greyson's nude body. Possessiveness flooded me, and I was suddenly moving. In a blink, I had Tara pinned against the wall.

Her wide eyes focused on me, and some of my hostility faded. Then she had to go and open her mouth.

"You fucking fae, he won't ever truly want you," Tara hissed, verbalizing the fear that I refused to face. Those words were a variation of the thoughts simmering under the surface.

Fisting my hand, I let it fly.

I could throw a punch. It had been one of the many things

Cosmo taught me, and while I'd socked a cocky guy here or there in my lifetime, I'd never put this much force behind it.

Blood splattered as Tara's head ricochet off my fist and hit the wall behind her. She blinked blearily for a second before her lip curled and she regained her senses. Before I could brace myself, she swept her leg out and knocked my feet out from under me.

Taken by surprise, I yelped when I hit the ground.

Familiar, rough hands gripped me and helped me regain my balance, but I quickly tried to shove past him. I had a lot of bruises I needed to get payback for. And now that I had the strength, I wasn't backing down.

I evaded Greyson's hold in a quick movement and lunged for Tara. I wrapped my hands around her throat and held on tight like I was wrangling a bull.

Claws sunk into my hands and scratched my skin, but I just pressed harder and used her own move against her. Her face gradually turned redder and redder.

Sweeping my leg under hers, I didn't let my grip off as she toppled to the ground. I took her down with more force than I'd meant to and winced at the crack in the floor.

"Sorry about that," I huffed back at Greyson. I dared a peek at him, only to find him gazing at me in awe, pride, and an awful lot of lust.

Unfortunately, it was the distraction Tara needed. She maneuvered her arm between mine and jerked her elbow up, breaking my grip. I grunted at the sharp numb-like pain move through my arms and let go.

Tara drew back her arm, and as I debated which way to roll, a large hand gripped her raised arm punishingly. "Do not touch her." She yelped and the loud crunch of bones reached my ears.

Tara screamed, desperately trying to yank away like a wounded animal.

Tara's eyes moved from the hand holding her up to the seriousness on Greyson's face.

Her expression twisted in genuine hurt, and I was surprised at the sympathetic pang that hit me. I scowled harshly as she scurried away with a defeated, lovelorn expression. I ground my teeth so hard, I wondered why they hadn't turned to dust by now.

A cool caress swiped over my naked shoulder, and I half-heartedly covered my bare chest as I climbed to my feet. I met Greyson's concerned expression before turning to leave.

"I'll make sure she's long gone before morning," he murmured and slid his hands around my waist. A heaviness on my chest receded at his touch, but I remain tensed.

"She seems genuinely hurt. She really cares about you," I said, hating how jealous I sounded.

"She understood what getting involved with me meant. The only person I need to apologize to is you. You shouldn't have had to deal with her shit. She should have never been allowed to stay here."

My muscles relaxed, and I let him draw me back. The words and gentle kisses to my cheek softened me.

"What if she's right?"

What if he didn't truly want me?

"She's not." Greyson nipped my ear. "I'll kill her right now —give the order and I'll snap her neck."

"Woah, tiger, chill."

I tried to pull away and he scowled.

"Stay with me," he whispered. I didn't fight as he drew me

to his bed. "You're the only one that's ever been allowed in my room."

"Oh, yeah?" I murmured, inching closer to him. The lines of our bodies pressed together tightly.

He hummed. "Unnaturals are very protective of their space."

A pleased pinch wiggled in my chest.

"Good," I whispered. He drew me tight to his chest.

CHAPTER 28
CAMILLA

You were sleeping, and I didn't want to wake you. Your wolf man woke me up at the crack of dawn. Hopefully by being in the middle of nowhere I won't make any stupid decisions. Talk later.

I BLINKED AT ELIZA'S TEXT. WHAT DID SHE MEAN, stupid decisions? My eyebrow flicked up, and I dialed her, wanting the answer asap. The phone rang and rang. I gazed down at my cell with a scowl. She must have sketchy reception. I placed my phone on the night stand.

I slipped from the bed, feeling off. It was a looming sense of something being wrong. I shook off my odd thoughts and hunted for my clothes before heading to the bathroom, needing to get cleaned off.

Fortunately, Greyson had his own so I didn't have to slink out of the room. The décor was simple yet elegant. The accent color a deep brown that contrasted well with the white surfaces. The shower head was a dream, the water gently pelted my skin.

Last night's memories flickered through my head, and I found myself grinning at the pristine shower tiles.

Finishing up, I dried off and tugged on my clothes from yesterday. I wondered how it was going to work between Greyson and me.

I was undeniably attracted to him, that wasn't the issue, but that whole mate thing . . .

My stomach clenched. He spoke of mates with reverence. Making it seem permanent. I didn't know everything about what being mates entailed, so it was making me more confused.

All I knew? I wasn't ready to jump in, regardless of how he made me feel. But I wasn't opposed to taking it slow, maybe dating for a while.

My face hurt from how hard I was smiling. Warmth in my chest swirled.

Finishing with my hair, I cracked the door open but froze when I heard Tara's voice on the other side.

"I don't fucking care! I put him in front of everything. I waited and waited while he overlooked me except when it was convenient to him."

"He wants you out," Daniel said calmly. I tensed and froze so they wouldn't catch me.

"Where am I supposed to go?" Tara asked, her voice cracking. I bit my lip hard, trying to distract myself from sympathizing with her.

"He said Tristin will take you in."

"Take me in," Tara repeated with a snort. "Like I'm a cast-off orphan."

"Just pack your shit, Tara. You're a big girl. You were looking after yourself just fine before. Greyson said you could take the Audi in the barn."

Tara scoffed. "A sendoff pity gift." A jingle of keys hit the porcelain counter.

"It's not like you have a car," Daniel said evenly.

I felt a mix of emotions. Happiness that he was making her go away, and odd possessiveness that he was giving her a damn car. I pushed that away.

If it made her go away faster, then all the better.

But I still didn't like it.

"Where is he?"

"He's not here, he went to turn in the fae to Tristin."

I tensed. The fae to Tristin? What did that mean?

"So he *is* going through with it." The relief in Tara's voice made my stomach turn. "I guess the only good thing is he must have seduced information out of her before giving her over."

Seducing me for information? I struggled to connect the dots, but everything came to me in a snap. Tara's interrogation, my refusal to talk, and the sudden change in how he treated me.

It was all to get information. He admitted it to me. That's what he'd wanted, but it wasn't until it came from someone else that it hit me like a truck.

Another thought popped into my head, we'd never been waiting for a witch to heal Cory. It was all a trick to keep me in place until they handed me over. That's why she'd suddenly "backed out."

All the lies filled my head, and I almost fell to my knees until I registered Daniel's next words.

"He's not handing his mate over. He's handing her friend over."

Wait . . . What?

He was handing over Eliza?

Surely he wouldn't do that. He had to have known how much that would hurt me.

I backed from the door and grabbed my cell again, trying Eliza, but it was no good. I flipped to the app to find friends, glad we'd all connected the features to each other's phones. The little dots lit up.

Thea seemed to be at her boyfriend's place. Rosalind was deep in the mountains. And Eliza . . . was nowhere near Rosalind's dot.

I brushed my wet hair back and clicked on Eliza's dot for the directions to her location. What to do?

Tara's car keys!

I inched back to the cracked doors and heard their voices moving up the stairs. Probably to pack her shit. I pulled my clothes on and slipped out, creeping to the kitchen where I swiped the keys and ran to the front door.

I practically flew... I was faster now, moving with a speed that was difficult for my brain to comprehend.

I moved to the barn at the farthest side of the house. It was huge and squat. When I pushed open the door, I found out why.

A row of vehicles lined the barn. I was by no means a car person, but I knew expensive when I saw it. There were even two of those antique old-fashioned trucks in the lineup. I eyed the lock on the gate that opened the big barn doors and tugged with no success. Shrugging, I took in the cherry red Audi and fought off the need to kick it and instead slid in.

I set up the directions to lead me to Eliza. It was a push start, so I revved it on with a grimace.

"Fancy," I said bitterly. I eyed the locked gate and grinned, stomping on the pedal with my beloved boots.

Wood exploded all around, but I didn't let loose on the car, forcing it toward the main road, the gravel flying everywhere. I checked my rearview mirror.

Daniel and Tara stood gaping near the front door. Shaking off his shock, Daniel burst into fur, and I stepped on it harder.

Ignoring my tail, I followed the directions of the phone as it guided me off the property.

I was coming, Eliza.

CHAPTER 29
GREYSON

THE REDHEAD'S EYES FLICKERED BEHIND THE CLOSED eyelids, and she jerked against the chains binding her limbs together.

Fuck, the dosage was too low.

Fortunately, the meeting spot was nearby. I revved my truck and pulled it into park. The engine hissed when I shut it off. Her eyes flashed open and she inhaled sharply.

I slipped out of my truck and rounded to open her side as she shook off the drug mixture that worked on fae. Once I had the door open, I wrapped my hand around the end of the witch-spelled chains pressing into her wrists.

She craned her head to peer into the cup holder where the syringe was and her eyes widened.

"What did you do to me?" she spat.

Irritation made my teeth snap together and a growl slipped free.

"Let's go. They're waiting." I tugged on the chain lightly. Even though I was about to hand her over, I didn't want to hurt her. She was my mate's friend.

If you cared about that you wouldn't be doing this.

I sneered at the inner voice.

There was no choice, we needed access to Faerie. It was her or my mate.

"Who's waiting?" Eliza said in a low tone, fear causing her voice to tremble.

That caused the increasingly uncomfortable guilt to lash out in my chest abruptly.

Only option.

With a hard yank, I pulled her out, but gave her enough time to catch herself before I continued in the direction Tristin waited.

Eliza stumbled after me. She grunted and I sensed her resolve before she charged at me. I sighed when she bounced off with a pain filled yelp.

I could see now why she and my mate got along so well.

"You're practically human right now. These." I shook the chains. "Stifle your Unnatural abilities."

Eliza scoffed, but I didn't bother waiting as she wrapped her head around that. My feet crunched over the foliage as I pulled the cussing fae after me.

"There you are," Tristin said. I met his eyes. Dominance seeped from his pores, but I didn't turn away.

I pulled Eliza up next to me.

"I brought her."

Tristin's eyes flicked over the girl, pausing over the pointed ears.

"Thank you, Greyson. I'll keep you appraised when we find a way into Faerie."

I nodded curtly and stilled.

"What will you with to her?"

Tristin's eyebrows furrowed. "I don't know yet, but the witches said there's a way to use fae to get to a portal."

That didn't tell me what they were going to do to her. My jaw worked and I pulled at the collar of my shirt.

"She's going to kill you, dog," Eliza snapped. I tensed and a tick started up in my cheek.

Tristin addressed the werewolf to my left.

"Go put her with the other one."

The gray haired *were* took a step forward and my internal hackles rose. He sneered at Eliza. There was something off about this fucker. I curled my lip at him.

I would have snapped his neck if he were looking at Camilla that way.

Camilla. Would she really hate me if I did this?

Yes.

My shoulders bunched. The eight *weres* stood in a semi-circle behind Tristin, eyes glinting with evil. Two of them shifted from foot to foot, nostrils flared.

This is a fucking stupid idea.

I'd held on to a pointless idea of revenge for too long. I didn't care about any of that anymore.

Camilla was enough. No, she was more than enough.

Straightening, I met Tristin's gaze head-on and pulled the girl behind me. "No."

She exhaled shakily.

"What do you mean?" The alpha jerked in surprise.

"I mean no. I'm not giving her over." I inclined my head to Eliza. "Let's go."

That's where I fucked up. I never should have looked away from them. I'd underestimated his desperation. A body barreled into me. I grunted and went flying into a tree.

The trunk snapped at the onslaught. I grunted from the impact and rolled to my feet. Narrowing my eyes, I growled. The guy that had been about to grab Eliza was dragging her away.

Fuck.

I pushed my shift forward. My body cracked and stretched until I was on all fours facing another wolf. I lunged at him and tossed him to the side. Dashing forward, my progress was halted when another wolf slammed into my side.

Twisting in the dirt, I shoved to my feet and found myself surrounded by three wolves. I snapped my teeth and lunged as they all rushed me.

CHAPTER 30
CAMILLA

I SLOWED TO A STOP WHEN I NEARED ELIZA'S DOT. I was glad the sun was out because it didn't take me long to pick out Greyson's truck sitting in a dirt lot in the middle of the forest. I pulled up behind it and hurried to whip open the door.

Empty.

My lips tightened, and I looked down at my phone. The little dot told me Eliza was here. I shoved open the back doors and found her phone on the floor, the missed calls lighting up the screen. I clenched my hand and let it fly into Greyson's precious truck. The car door screeched. If I had more time, I would have taken a bat to it.

A muffled scream sounded. I froze and strained to hear. There was fighting going on from all sides, but that scream was familiar. I rushed in its direction, running through foliage.

Eliza struggled to escape as she was toted to the van sitting far within the trees. Eliza wiggled over his shoulder, but he wrestled her into the vehicle.

Time to move. I inched around the other side of the trees,

wanting to catch the guy holding Eliza off guard. The doors were shoved open as he leaned in and shoved at Eliza.

He didn't count on being attacked. *I* didn't even see it coming.

A large form slammed into him from inside the truck, and they fell back in a heap, Eliza right next to them.

I took that as my cue and charged toward her. The wolf on the floor tried to push up, but I kicked his head, and he fell facedown like a brick. Out.

Pressing my finger to my lips to shush Eliza, I listened for anyone coming, but thankfully, the only noise I heard was snarling and shouting. The cacophony was too muddled for me to make anything out.

I reached for her, and she struggled to her feet with my help.

A familiar voice snapped at us. "Let me out of these."

Eliza and I turned and gaped down at the tightly bound fae at our feet. I knew him.

Kean, the onyx-haired fae who had been in charge of making sure we ate during our captivity.

"The dickwad?" Eliza asked, using the name we'd call him behind his back.

"The dickwad," I confirmed and kicked his thigh. He hissed and glowered up at me.

"We need to get out of here. Get these off me," Eliza said quickly, shaking her chains. I yanked the bindings at her arms, but quickly retreated with a frustrated hiss. Of course, they'd tied her with something not easily released.

"They remove any abilities. You're as weak as a human when you touch it," Kean drawled mockingly

"Shut it." Eliza narrowed her eyes at Kean.

I was going to have to carry her and run. She nodded,

understanding what we were going to have to do. We were on the same wavelength, so she pressed into my back when I crouched. Eliza made sure to keep her chains away from me, and I easily picked her up. I gripped her thighs, and she held onto my neck with the side of her arms.

"How'd you find me?"

I patted my pocket. "The app. I'm glad we got all of our phones connected to it."

I stepped away from the struggling fae, but before I could escape with Eliza.

My legs flew out from under me. Eliza sailed out of my hold. I rolled across the ground, scraping my arms and face.

In the next instant, a heavy body landed on me, and then the manic-eyed male wrapped his hands around my neck.

I threw out my arms in panic, trying to push him off me. Our strength matched each other, but he was heavier and practiced so he had me still in moments.

A rage-filled snarl resonated, sending shivers down my neck. The body on top of me was ripped off, and I caught sight of Greyson's wolf form as he tore into the wolf who had been choking me.

"Get up, stupid girl." Kean dragged me up. His hands were still locked in the chains.

Another massive male charged Kean and punched him so hard, he smashed into a tree. The psycho turned his attention to me now that Kean was out of the way. I tensed, prepared to run, but he was much quicker than I was. Not to mention, good at fighting.

Psycho wolf wrapped chains around my arms, tightening and twisting them around my wrists. As soon as the cool metal touched my skin, my muscles weakened, and I helplessly wiggled beneath him.

A dagger flew through the air and thumped into the arm holding me down. In a swish of movement, a petite woman kicked the werewolf away from me. I gaped up at the beauty looking down at me with determined eyes.

"I'm Gracelyn. Rae sent me to help."

Words escaped me. *Rae* sent her . . .?

She helped me stand and kicked away the chains that I managed to wiggle out of, then pulled Eliza over her shoulder. It looked funny since Gracelyn was a tiny little thing.

She gripped my wrist and pulled me to run with her. I peered back, my heart thumping hard against my chest as Greyson fought the pack of wolves.

CHAPTER 31
GREYSON

I buried my teeth into the male who had been choking my mate. Red filled my vision. I'd kill every last one of them for daring to touch her.

Before I could tear open his throat, my prey was suddenly dragged away from under me. I growled at Tristin, who held his hands up.

Blood dried on his body. I peeled my lips back, not wanting to listen to his bullshit.

The dark-haired male fae swiped a cell phone from the ground before taking off into the woods. I could have easily chased after him considering he was still hampered by the chains, but I had better things to worry about.

"Let's not start a feud," Tristin said calmly, eyes narrowing. He was a strong wolf, and we were even in strength. It would take effort, but I could end him if I gave it my all.

I wanted his blood. These were his wolves, and he'd let this happen. I inched closer, curling my lip up.

"Look, I'll leave your fae alone. I don't need her anyway, but

I have to catch the one that's taking off," Tristin said. "There have been enough deaths."

Reason filtered into my animalistic need to take him down. I lifted my head. Camilla. Where had she gone? Frustration and fear flooded me.

Was she hurt?

"They ran that way with another of their kind," Tristin said slowly and pointed to the side.

I narrowed my eyes at the alpha and tore off toward my car. I shifted next to my truck, and my eyebrow went up at the dent in the side. I peered closer and made out the small knuckles. My lips twitched, but the seriousness of the situation returned.

Camilla knew I'd lied to her.

I grabbed the keys in the cupholder. She had to give me a chance to explain.

Either way, I'd never leave her. She was stuck with me.

I revved the engine, and as I backed up, there was a thump and the screech of metal on metal. I winced and peeled to the side.

It was the red Audi I'd slammed into. The car I fucking hated.

Tara had taken a liking to it, so I associated it with her. That's why I wanted her to take it. I wanted nothing of hers in my house.

I banished all thoughts of Tara from my head and worked on finding out where my Camilla had run off to.

CHAPTER 32
CAMILLA

"Rae really sent you?" Eliza asked, looking at the fae sitting on the edge of our couch.

Gracelyn nodded once. "My mission is to check on each of you to ensure your safety. I am to take as long as I must to be positive you will all be fine. I am also here to warn you about other Unnaturals who will try to kill you."

"Yeah, we caught on to that bit," Eliza said sarcastically. I followed her eyes to the chains we managed to get off her. They sat on the coffee table.

Now that I was home, sitting on the couch, the adrenaline had made its way out of my system, and in its place came the pain. Betrayal stung like a fresh wound. I squeezed my eyelids shut. I was not going to cry.

"Do you know about mates?" I asked Gracelyn.

"Some," she responded cautiously.

"How does it work?"

"Fae mates recognize each other once they've touched skin to skin. As long as you both are meant to be, you will know with that one touch. You may even get the barest hint of each other's emotions." Her expression tightened.

I mulled that over. "What if you're not fae? Does it work the same?"

Gracelyn shook her head. "No, animal Unnaturals have the confirmation of their mate once they are intimate with the person. There are also physiological changes." The knotting and half-shift Greyson had undergone. "Vampires recognize their mates from tasting blood directly from the skin. That's simply knowing who your mate is. It's different to cementing bonds. A blood exchange is needed to complete their mating."

"What does 'completing' it mean?" Eliza asked, on edge.

"Binding mates' lives together. I don't know much about other species." Gracelyn shrugged.

I rubbed my eyes.

"What about mates from different species? Like cross matings," I asked slowly. Eliza's surprised eyes swung to mine, horror and sadness filling them.

"Well, there isn't much information on that." Gracelyn frowned. "I believe it varies and depends on what species we're speaking of."

Greyson had changed when we screwed once I'd matured. That was physical change . . . Was the bite . . . then the warmth that traveled through my veins when I bit his lip and tasted his blood?

"Fuck," I muttered and froze when realization dawned.

They turned questioning eyes to me, and I swept my hair aside so they could take in the faintest bite mark. Gracelyn's eyes widened. I'd gotten a look at it when I took a shower. It was a healed row of canine-esque teeth imprinted within my skin.

"Wolf dude," Eliza said, tsking.

"After I turned fae and we started getting down and dirty"—I almost laughed at the scandalized expression on Gracelyn's face—"the physical changes happened while he was in me."

"Maybe in regard to animal Unnaturals, the mating takes on their characteristics. So you had to participate in *certain* acts to find out," Gracelyn theorized and flushed. Eliza and I exchanged a look. We were definitely going to corrupt this fae.

"Well, whatever. I'm not speaking to the liar." My words made me ache at the thought of not seeing him. I stabbed my fingers into my hair. Dammit, Greyson.

Eliza's concern shouted at me, but I refused to meet her look.

"Plot twist with Kean being there, right?" Eliza said dryly. And that's why she and I clicked so well. She knew when I needed to be distracted.

"Seriously," I responded. "I never liked how he watched Rosalind."

"Rosalind? I was going to say Selina. I mean, she did bring it on when she started all that flirting, but she was trying to find a way to get her sister out."

We went quiet at the mention of Karen, the young girl who didn't make it out with us. None of us would dare judge the fact that Selina had been willing to use sex to get out of there. She had been the only one with a young sister at risk.

"He was playing with Selina's hope, but he wanted Rosalind," I claimed. Even if *he* couldn't tell.

It'd taken me a while to get a read on Kean, but when I had, I realized the yearning in his eyes was for the woman he always snarled at and called "mouse."

These Unnatural guys really had a shitty way of showing they wanted you.

"Well, thank God she's in the middle of nowhere. She would not have been able to handle seeing that dickwad," Eliza commented dryly, and I snorted.

A hard knock on the front door sent me to my feet. I sped to the door with the girls at my heels. Opening it, a small part of me expected Greyson, but I was more shocked by who waited.

"Cosmo!" I exclaimed and pulled him inside the threshold before throwing my arms around his neck.

"Hey, little sis," he murmured into my hair.

I pulled back and had to crane my neck to see him properly. He was a year older than me, and we looked nothing alike.

Where I was tan, he was pale. Even our hair was the opposite. His was a soft blond that contrasted with my dark hair.

"Your grip has gotten stronger. Have you been working out?" He grunted, and I loosened my hold quickly.

"What are you doing here?" The rest of my question cut off with a scream as someone shoved me to the side and pinned Cosmo to the wall.

Greyson.

Greyson pushed his forearm into Cosmo's neck. I cried out and gripped his arm to push him away.

"Stop," I yelled and punched his shoulder. He didn't even budge. "He's my brother."

Greyson dropped Cosmo just as quickly as he appeared. My chest heaved from anger. My brother was not a small guy, so he must have been confused as to why he didn't stand a chance against Greyson.

"What are you doing here?"

"I came to retrieve you."

"I'm not some toy you can fetch and use however you like," I said slowly.

Greyson's eyes widened, and he shook his head. "It's not like that—"

"I don't want to hear it," I retorted. "I want you out. Forget about me, I'm done with this." My heart wrenched, and I swallowed hard.

"No—"

"You've been lying to me this entire time," I interrupted. "I don't trust you, and I never will, and no relationship can survive that, so leave."

Greyson's face twisted with pain before it hardened with determination. "I won't let you go. We belong to each other."

"Tell me why. What are you all after?"

"The Queen." He rushed on when he saw I was going to interrupt. "We'd been wronged. Every Unnatural wants revenge, and there's a search for ways to get into Faerie."

Cosmo opened his mouth, but Eliza shushed him, and he thankfully listened to her.

"You goddamned bastards. I told you the Queen was as innocent as me. What would revenge do for you now anyway?" I scoffed with disdain.

Greyson's lips tightened. "It stopped meaning anything to me now that I have you."

A small part inside me, one I was trying hard to kill, knew he'd been motivated by that hate in his heart for fae and he would have done anything to relieve that. And his vengeance was how he'd made it easier to cope with his guilt. All I did was point at the door behind him.

Greyson looked like he wanted to add more. He dragged his palm over his face. Opened his mouth, then closed it.

With a final look that promised this wasn't over, he turned on his heels with a growl. I slammed the door behind him. I stared at the ground, trying to piece together my fragile state of mind.

"Rae was hoping you could get me a cell phone and teach me how to use it," Gracelyn said to Eliza.

"No problem, that can be arranged quickly." Eliza cleared her throat. "Let's go, Cosmo."

Their voices trailed farther away. I fought the urge to slide down the wall in tears. I wanted to just fall to the floor, but I inhaled sharply and turned to follow everyone.

"I'm fine," I muttered with a scowl when they turned their concerned eyes on me. They were back on the couch. Eliza gripped Cosmo's arm.

"What the hell!" I exclaimed when I saw Cosmo's arm bleeding profusely. As soon as I noticed it, the coppery scent made sense.

"Did that guy have a knife? I didn't even see it." Greyson's claws must have been out when he pinned him. "You need to change your taste in men, Cam. Damn weirdo, what was he going on about anyway?"

I rolled my eyes to hide the pain in them. Cosmo's face twisted, and I inched forward as he stretched out his arm. I needed him healed. I hated seeing him hurt. Even though he was older, I'd always felt protective of him. I carefully examined his wounds up to take stock of the damage.

"Eliza, can you get something so I can clean this?"

Taking a seat beside him, I took the cloth Eliza handed me. The damp material absorbed his blood until the jagged wound was easier to see. Flesh was split and ragged. My stomach churned. It started at the inside of his elbow and stretched to his wrist.

It looked like it hurt so bad.

Panic prickled my chest. He needed stitches. I pressed the towel to the seeping blood.

Crap. This was too much. I set the drenched cloth aside and grabbed a fresh one. It must have hit a vein.

"Here's a disinfectant cream. I'll go get another hand towel."

Gracelyn shuffled as she watched me. Squeezing the tube, I slathered the ointment on my trembling fingers.

I started at the edge of his wound, making sure to get as much as I could. Cosmo hissed and tried to jerk away.

A knot built in my throat. I hated hurting him. He needed to be fine. My brain took me to the worst case scenario. Fear made my heart race and heat spread through my chest and through my nerve endings.

The flesh started knitting together under my eyes. A burning sensation intensified and kept me frozen on him. I cried out, a wave of weakness making me slump. The sting of pain on my arm numbed me.

Heat faded from my body. A small portion of his flesh was half knit together. My arm began stinging intensely and I rubbed the ghost pain of the wound and swayed.

It was getting harder and harder to keep my eyelids open.

Cosmo grunted, and his hands grasped my shoulders as I fell forward.

"What goddamned happened?" Cosmo's eyes went wide from shock, his already pale skin turning paler. He gaped down at the portion the gash had semi-healed at his wrist.

"You're a healer," Gracelyn's voice sounded far away.

I groaned and sank deeper into the couch, meeting Eliza's eyes. I didn't have the energy to tell her what I wanted, but she read it in my gaze. The last I heard before I passed out was Eliza explaining the world we found ourselves a part of to my brother.

CHAPTER 33
CAMILLA

Cosmo had amazingly taken the news of what I was with minimal panic . . . With Eliza talking him down. I'd been too busy rolling my eyes. He was still here, and I didn't see him leaving anytime soon because he wanted to keep an eye on me. My big brother was a pain in the ass I'd never wish away.

It'd been a week and a half without Greyson.

He'd come knocking every day, but I never answered the door, instead choosing to hunker down in my room. But the distance weighed on me more and more each day. The only indirect contact I'd allowed was when he had goddamned flowers delivered on my birthday. There was no card, nothing, just a gray wolf stuffed animal accompanying the huge bouquet.

I frowned at my new cell phone. I'd attempted to track down the one I'd lost, but my dot had disappeared. It stated inactivity from my account. I counted it as another loss.

I fell back into my bed and gazed at my ceiling. With my advanced hearing, I recognized someone approached my room. Sure enough, seconds later, the door opened and closed. It wasn't until the bed dipped beside me that I turned my head.

"I hate seeing you sad," Eliza mumbled.

"I'm not sad." She flicked an eyebrow up, and I huffed. "Fine. I'm sad. But I'll be fine."

"I'm sure you will." Eliza rubbed her face. "I know why you won't go to him, but you need to know something." She sighed. "Yeah, he's a liar and I know you hate those like a bad rash, but if you're also staying away from him because he handed me over. Then that shouldn't be a reason."

My brows furrowed.

"What do you mean it shouldn't be a reason? That's the main reason. How dare he try to do that to someone I love." My voice hitched.

"He changed his mind and told that other guy no. He started fighting all of them before they dragged me away."

I opened my mouth and snapped it shut.

"I don't want you to be sad. If you like the dog, go for it. I mean, if you think about it . . . it was kind of romantic that he didn't give you over. Even if it was at my expense." I snorted at her poorly timed joke. Eliza went quiet, and her hand squeezed mine. "At the very least, you need closure. It's like you're just waiting for him. Go end it for real, then we can move on properly from the dog-man experience."

"We?" I flicked an eyebrow up. Did she have a dog-man I didn't know about?

She coughed. "I meant you, but us in a solidarity thing." She blinked innocently. "We can get blackout drunk tonight. What do you say?"

I licked my lips. She had a point.

I shoved off the bed and tugged my boots on. "You're right. Plus, there's something I wanted to try."

"IT'S A BAD IDEA. You hardly made a dent in Cosmo's wound and you passed out for days." Eliza huffed. "This is cancer we're talking about!"

I shouldn't have let her drive me. I knew she'd have a fit.

"I've been practicing," I said, exasperated. As soon as I told her my plan, she kept arguing I was making the wrong decision. "He's just a boy, and I need to try. Anyway, now that magic is back, he just needs get to maturing age. I can help keep him alive until then."

She huffed and threw her hands up. I pointed the way to Ann's house, hoping I could get the healing done quickly.

Eliza's car slid to a stop and shut off.

Without hesitation, I jumped out and strode to the front door. It whipped open before I was able to knock a second time.

"Hey, Cindy," I said to the girl looking up at me with a grin. She came in for a hug. I made sure to be gentle.

"Cindy," Ann yelled frantically. A tall, lean man appeared behind her and curled his lip at me. I stepped back and held up my hands. "What are you doing here?"

I swallowed the sarcastic response. "I came to see Cory."

"No," she snapped. "You're the reason Alpha's been chewing everyone's head off whenever he's actually been around."

"Ann, just once. Then I'm leaving and you never have to see me again."

Her eyes flickered.

"Mom," Cindy murmured, confused by the antagonism.

Ann looked at her daughter and softened. "Fine, but just a second."

Ann cut off the man standing behind her when he moved to get in my way. I pushed past them, ignoring the male's glare, and rushed up the steps with my fae speed. I knocked on his door and didn't wait for a response as I pushed it open.

"Hey," he said weakly, the shadow under his eyes.

I perched next to him, pressing my lips together. Hopefully, I wasn't making it worse. "I came to check on you."

His brows furrowed and he tried to push up. "Don't strain yourself. Keep resting." I didn't need to bother saying anything because his body couldn't handle the strain and he fell back.

Sickness was heavy in the air. I swallowed hard. He looked half dead.

"Cory, would you trust me for a second?"

He blinked in confusion, but he nodded slowly. When I'd healed Cosmo, I had to touch the direct wound. I didn't know how lung cancer worked, but I figured I needed to be as close to his lungs as possible.

I tugged off the blanket covering his chest and settled my hands over him. I could hear the wheeze.

Closing my eyes, I breathed deep. I tried mimicking the sensations and emotions I'd had when I'd healed Cosmo.

The desire, the fear, the image—I pulled on all of it.

Heat flooded me, and I trembled. My hands heated to a painful degree. Cory cried out under me, and I heard steps running in our direction but I ignored everyone and focused.

My chest began to ache, a heavy sensation settling in my lungs. My breath came in short bursts, and I coughed, but I refused to let go. My body shook with pain, then I was torn away from him. I had no energy, so I hit the closet. Wood burst and cracked under me. I grunted at the impact as Ann faced me, her lips peeled back.

"Mom, no," Cory yelled. His voice had barely been a wheeze earlier, but now it was a touch clearer. My mouth dropped when he was able to push up in the bed. His expression strained and he stumbled and fell to his knees. Dragging himself over to me, he panted and scooted to where I watched him. The room faded from my vision as my chest remained tight from pressure. Tears filled his eyes as he gripped my arm.

"That's all I can do for now. It's not much . . ." I breathed, sprawled on the floor, unable to move. "If we keep doing little healings like that, maybe we can keep you alive until you change?"

My words slurred and my eyes fluttered shut.

"Thank you." Gratitude and exhaustion shone through his tone.

"My baby," Ann whispered, and then she was sobbing. I was able to peel an eyelid open to watch her arms wrap around Cory from behind as he kept hold of me.

"Camilla." Was that Greyson? My head rolled to the side, and everything went black.

CHAPTER 34
CAMILLA

Voices filtered through my semi-conscious brain. I swayed. Was I being carried?

I couldn't make my body react to anything I was demanding of it. Last I remembered, I was healing Cory and then I'd imagined Greyson's voice.

There was a crunch of gravel. Another set of steps stomped next to him.

"Give her to me, and we'll get out of your way," Eliza demanded.

"No."

Eliza yelled and cursed at him with various profanities. Something creaked, and cool air brushed my face.

"I won't hurt her." Greyson sighed. "I did want to apologize for tricking you."

Eliza grunted. My eyes fluttered open, and I groaned.

"She's awake!" she exclaimed.

Greyson shuddered and gripped me tighter. He pushed into his bedroom and set me on the mattress.

Eliza turned mulish and crossed her arms. "I'm not leaving."

He shuffled her back and slammed the door in her face. She was undoubtedly pissed, but she'd wait unless I told her it was okay if she left.

Surrounded by his scent, I melted into the cushions.

"New bed?" I rasped as he moved toward me. His serious eyes took me in. "I just need to rest."

I clutched my chest, the remnant pain still present. He eyed me, and his face tightened. He grasped one of my hands and squeezed.

"Thank you for helping Cory, but I need you never to do that again," he said seriously. I blinked at him with confusion. "You collapsed," he rasped, exhaling sharply. "Don't you understand you're the most important thing to me?"

The fracture in my chest trembled.

"Why did you lie to me?" I voiced what had been bothering me every second of the last week. The vulnerability of the question made me look away.

"I know I fucked up, but you need to get through your head that it's not this connection to you. Or the fact that we're bound together as mates. I liked you before that. I've liked you since you strutted up to me in that bar."

My heart thundered in my ears as I struggled to make sense of his words.

This was the moment of truth. I could reject him and go on with my life, trying to forget him even though the thought of him would haunt me forever. Or I could give it one more try. Eliza's words resonated through me.

"I love you," Greyson rasped. "I promise to never betray your trust."

Pressing my lips together, I eyed him doubtfully.

The two parts of me battled it out, all I knew was I didn't want to hurt again.

"Please. Just feel my sincerity." He picked up my hand and pressed it to his chest.

I licked my lips and let our bond open. His love flooded me. I squeezed my eyelids tightly.

Uncertainty, fear, self hatred . . . it was all woven under the cloud of lust and love. The emotions whirled together, and my throat tightened painfully. He'd really hurt me. The lies—all of it. I didn't know if I could get over it, but . . . I wanted to try, because I loved him. For the most part, I understood his actions, but that didn't mean they didn't hurt.

I hated regretting more than anything and if I didn't give us *one* shot to see if I could accept him, I would regret it. I'd never been one to go against my gut, and my gut wanted me to take the leap. With a sigh, I gave in to his embrace.

"I've been setting everything up for you here." He forced me to look at him, and my eyebrows furrowed. "I'm having a barn built for you. I want you to be able to fill it with whatever animals you want."

I gaped up at him and started shaking my head. He pressed his finger to my lips before I could speak. He nuzzled into the crook of my neck, moaning against my throat. "My Boots."

I softened and slapped his shoulder. "Please find another endearment."

The door slammed open.

Eliza stood there, furious, her red hair puffed up around her head.

"Shit, woman. Give them privacy," Daniel yelled and grabbed her around the waist and tugged her back.

"Let me go, dog." She socked his arm, but then the door shut. I tensed and turned to Greyson in worry.

"He won't hurt her," he reassured me.

I pressed my lips together and nodded slowly, choosing to take the leap of faith.

"Where were we?" I murmured and fused my lips to his.

CHAPTER 35
CAMILLA

I woke with a gasp and arched on the bed, my fingers digging into the mattress under me. I took in Greyson's dark hair moving between my legs as he licked my pussy with smooth strokes. It was how I was woken up every time I stayed the night at his place. And I couldn't say I hated it.

Whimpering, I reached down and combed my hands through his hair, forcing him harder on my clit.

He growled and gripped my ass to pull me closer to his wet tongue. My chest rose sharply and caught when he sucked my clit between his lips and sucked in a hard drag. His finger crept up and slipped inside my pussy.

Then a second. I thrashed as he moved them inside me, thrusting them deep.

"Live with me," he demanded more than asked. A smile spread my lips. This was my favorite game. He'd pushed me to the edge, demanding things of me, but I always managed to resist because he never withheld anything from me for long.

All it took was one whispered "please", and he gave it to me.

It had been a month that we'd been seeing each other, and

every second together was perfect, while every second apart made me anxious. I'd already been debating telling him yes to his more serious questions, the ones he asked me every night we were together.

"Mm, do I have this to look forward to every morning?" I rasped huskily.

"Not just mornings." He growled, and the vibration went straight to my core.

"How can I resist?" I responded, and he tensed and deepened his licks.

"Don't resist." Greyson continued his onslaught, and I groaned as my orgasm swelled.

"Okay," I breathed finally. His head popped up, lips wet with my desire. "Yes." Utter happiness reflected back at me, and my chest tightened with all the love I had for him.

"I'll send someone to move all of your things." He pushed up as if to leave, and I sat up and grabbed his thick arms. I grinned at him.

He was always looking out for me, making sure every need was met before I knew I needed it. Even his pack was coming around to my presence, although I thought that had more to do with their complete respect for their alpha. Ann had even warmed up to me.

"We can discuss semantics later."

I huffed breathlessly when he playfully nipped my lip. Every hair on my body rose and I flopped onto my back.

He grinned wide and slid back down my body to attack my pussy with fervor. I cried and whimpered, close to the edge, but then he lifted his head again. I slammed my hand on the bedding and glared down at him.

"Marry me? The human way?"

I'd been waiting for this question, it always came on the heels of his earlier one. I forced my expression clear and yanked his head back down to my pussy, stifling his next words.

Grey flicked his tongue and swirled it around the bud. My toes curled, lips parting on a gasp as he sucked it between his lips.

The orgasm tingled over my flesh and warmth spread from my belly down to my toes. I couldn't stop thrashing my head side to side as I arched closer to his mouth. He gave me exactly what I asked for and thrust his tongue into my sheath, lapping up my juices. My ears rang as the wall of heat crashed into me, engulfing me and dragging me under.

"Grey," I cried as my pussy throbbed against his ravenous mouth.

THANK YOU FOR READING!

Visit my website for more book information and be sure to join my reader group and follow my social media platforms to keep up with my releases.

ACKNOWLEDGMENTS

I'm feeling redundant mentioning Gina Cortez, but I must!
Gina, I love you, girl. I hope we have many successful author
years ahead of us.
I've met so many wonderful writers that are always willing to
brainstorm with me and just be a support in general—
thank you!

Aaron, thank you for dealing with my writer moods and
tendencies.

Gracias a mis papas por todo. Los quiero.

ABOUT THE AUTHOR

Allie obsessively reads books featuring sexy, possessive heroes and headstrong heroines. So, it's no wonder characters just like that bustle to escape her imagination.

When she's not working away at her keyboard, she can be found in bed with a good book or bingeing Netflix.

www.ingramcontent.com/pod-product-compliance
Lightning Source LLC
Chambersburg PA
CBHW010751310726
48974CB00004B/875